Dear Librarians/Booksellers/Book Reviewers/Teachers/General
Custodians of the Sanctity of the Written Word,

Good afternoon/evening/midnight trip to the bathroom/
refrigerator/garbage can! My name is Kate McKinnon. I am
a sketch comedian, an enthusiastic but unsuccessful gardener,
and a onetime Little League umpire. Pro tip: It's best to be *rock-
solid* on the rules of softball before the caffeinated suburban
fathers fill the bleachers.

In my youth (and, let's face it, in my adulthood), I was, as
they say in English, "weird." I shared my room with both an
iguana AND a tank of Madagascar hissing cockroaches (not a
joke, ask my traumatized mother); after eating mussels mar-
inara at a seafood restaurant I insisted on bringing home the
shells for my collection; I went to school in a Peter Pan costume for a year, then the following year I switched to wearing
pipe cleaners in my braids to look like Pippi Longstocking; I
liked slime and goop and I said the wrong thing and I did weird
voices and made weird jokes and I had no friends, until I found
some girls that were into lizards and theater, and then I was off
to the races. I was one of the lucky ones.

My secret mission in everything I do is to give a private nod
to the next generation of weirdos—to make them feel less alone,
to make them feel like they *do*, in fact, have something important to contribute. If I were not already a sketch comedian, I
think that I would want to become a mad scientist living in a
crumbling Victorian mansion filled with sentient hermit crabs
and floating jellyfish, and I would start a school for girls who
were too weird for whatever environment they were born into,

and I would teach them what I know. And then the government would shut me down. But that's neither here nor there.

That's why I've written this story about three little misfits stuck in a repressive turn-of-the-century town and their bizarre mentor, Millicent Quibb. I wanted to create a world that little STEM girls and little theater girls alike could escape to, get lost in, be delighted by, and be inspired by—to go out and do their own experiments, strengthen their own sisterhoods, and fight their own battles. Our youth have been saddled with an uncertain future, riddled with problems not of their own making—the least we can do is teach them what we know, and give them the confidence to get out there and fix it.

Thank you so much for reading,

Kate McKinnon

THE
Millicent Quibb
School of Etiquette
for Young Ladies
of Mad Science

THE
Millicent Quibb
School of Etiquette
for Young Ladies
of Mad Science

By G. Edwina Candlestank *as told to*
KATE McKINNON

HARPERCOLLINS
CHILDREN'S BOOKS

First published in the United States of America by Little Brown and Company,
a division of Hachette Book Group Inc. in 2024
Published simultaneously in the United Kingdom by
HarperCollins *Children's Books* in 2024
HarperCollins *Children's Books* is a division of HarperCollins*Publishers* Ltd
1 London Bridge Street
London SE1 9GF

www.harpercollins.co.uk

HarperCollins*Publishers*
Macken House, 39/40 Mayor Street Upper
Dublin 1, DO1 C9W8, Ireland

1

ISBN 978-0-00-871065-1

Kate McKinnon and Alfredo Caceres assert the moral right to be identified as
the author and illustrator of the work respectively.

This is a work of fiction. Names, characters, places and incidents are the product
of the author's imagination or are used fictitiously. Any resemblance to
actual events, locales or persons, living or dead, is coincidental.

A CIP catalogue record for this title is available from the British Library.

Interior design by Karina Granda
Printed and bound in the UK using 100% renewable electricity at
CPI Group (UK) Ltd

This book contains FSC™ certified paper and other controlled sources
to ensure responsible forest management.

Find out more about HarperCollins and the environment at
www.harpercollins.co.uk/green

for my Mamarama—

joker, writer, speaker, thinker,
activist, iconoclast, total blast—

---

who encouraged me to march to the
beat of my own drum,

then bought me the drum,

drove me to marching lessons,

sewed the costume,

and cheered the whole time

·ANTIQUARIUM·

RHODECHUSSETTS, USA, 1911

Former capital of mad science of the northern hemisphere

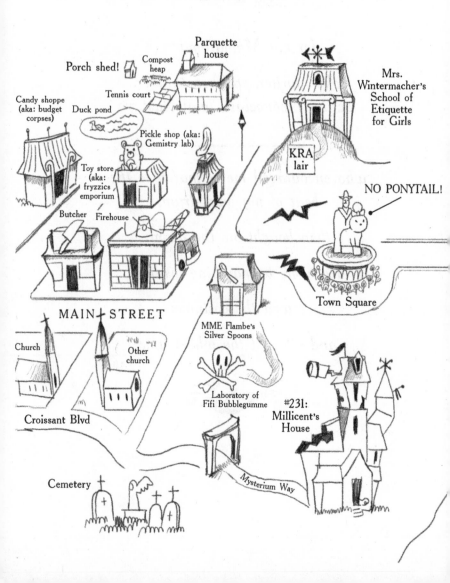

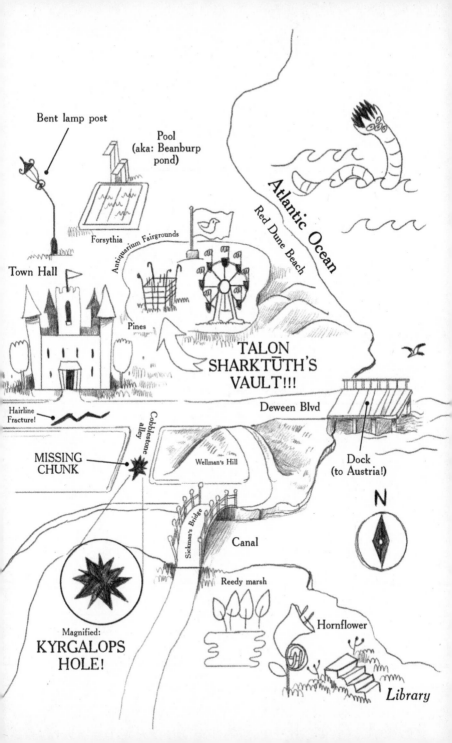

FOREWORD

GOOD EVENING. My name is Dr. G. Edwina Candlestank. I am a mad scientist, a prize-winning quiltist, and a one-time concert violist. Man, do I hate the viola.

I begin this book from my study, which is wood paneled and gorgeous. It was in this very study that my publisher, Mr. Bookman, called and said, "Dr. Candlestank, your adult books about mad science are not selling very well." And I said, "Well, crud in a tub! Why do you think that is?" And he said, "They're very dry. No one is going to buy a book called *The Unnatural Yams of Alberta: A History*." And I said, "You clown! That book is a page-turner!" And he said, "Why don't you write a book about mad science for the young?" And I said,

"Ugh, fine, but I can't type right now because my hands are lizard hands." And he said, "What do you mean?" And I said, "I just did an experiment with an iguana and now my hands are lizard hands and I can't hold a pen. Was I not clear?"

In any case, I got my human hands back and realized that Mr. Bookman was right. I MUST WRITE A BOOK ABOUT MAD SCIENCE FOR THE YOUNG, BECAUSE IT IS THE YOUNG WHO WILL SAVE US, AND INDEED MUST SAVE THEMSELVES. I think the best way to illustrate to you, dear reader, how you can become a young mad scientist, is to tell you about three children who did just that. One day they were ordinary, if ostracized, children in the snooty town of Antiquarium, and the next, they found themselves at the center of an infernal battle. Chances are you've never heard of this battle—of Gertrude, Eugenia, and Dee-Dee Porch, pupils of the Millicent Quibb School of Etiquette for Young Ladies of Mad Science, and their valiant fight against the nefarious Krenetics Research Association—but I guarantee you, had they not bothered, you would not be sitting there right now, wherever it is you're sitting.[1]

---

1 Or standing, though who reads standing up? Someone without a chair, I suppose. I do not presume to know your chair status.

This book is a record of their struggle, a struggle that is, of course...

ONGOING·

—**Dr. G. Edwina Candlestank**

P.S. This book has too many footnotes, and I know it. You do not have to read them, but you could if you had time on your hands. Though if you do have time on your hands, I suggest washing it off—it chafes the skin.

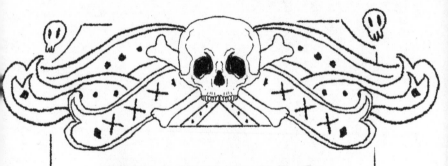

WARNING:

The situations contained in these books could cause:

Instant death

Extremely instant death (bad)

Semi-instant death (worse)

Burning in the upper extremities

Burning in the lower extremities

Permanent intestinal parasites

Being shrunk to the size of a seed

Sprouting plants from the top of the
     head and/or fingertips

Cauliflower ear

Crab foot

Quesadilla brain

Abdomen grenade

Wasting away

Heed my tale, I tell no fib
Beware the home of Millicent Quibb
She'll twist your skull until it's loose,
Then pickle your brain in lemon juice
Her hair is wild, her clothes are smelly
All coated with fish and rotted jelly
You needn't fear the witch's curse
Mad scientists like her are much, much worse
If you hope to grow up past eleven
Or have a birthday when you're seven
Or even make it past the crib
Beware the home of Millicent Quibb!

—children's rhyme,
Antiquarium and surrounding environs, 1911ish

CHAPTER 1

THE INVITATION

THE MYSTERIOUS INVITATIONS appeared on a Tuesday.

They appeared inside three backpacks belonging to three pupils at Mrs. Wintermacher's School of Etiquette for Girls, in the town of Antiquarium.[1]

No one saw who might have *put* them in the backpacks, because the backpacks were kept all day in the backpack

---

1 I tell you this because your journey to become a young mad scientist will probably begin with a mysterious invitation. Of course it could also begin with you finding a mysterious book of laboratory notes, a mysterious bag of medical instruments, or a mysterious store of stuff in jars. In the 1950s it was common to be snatched into a car by the FBI; in the '90s, chain e-mail. But paper invitations are making a comeback—which is good, because they bring a greater sense of fun—so you should be prepared.

room, and that afternoon the students were busy in the demonstration room. What were they doing in the demonstration room? They were watching a demonstration. Keep up!

Mrs. Wintermacher, the proprietress of the school, was demonstrating how to sit on a velvet fainting couch.

"Let us begin," she said. "Sitting is, as you know, the delicate art of not standing. In Antiquarium, if you attempt to sit without the proper training, you may be wounded, or worse, look weird."

She pursed her gray lips, struggling to balance all the exotic feathers and fruits and taxidermied animals atop her enormous hat.

"Today we tackle the hardest couch of all: the velvet fainting couch."

"Oooooh!" gasped the pupils.

"Yes, velvet is a cruel mistress. There are no fewer than eighty-five different poses that you must memorize for this couch. We'll begin with the simplest, which is 'Upright Sit with Straight Back,' and gradually we'll work our way up to more difficult maneuvers, such as 'Fainting During Public Waltz' and 'Laughing at the Admiral's Joke.' I'll begin."

Mrs. Wintermacher sat straight as a sword on the velvet couch while all the pupils watched with rapt attention.

Well, not all. Not...

THE PORCH SISTERS·

Brain: Big ideas, bigger ideas

Hair: Too tall

Mouth: Weird jokes (when nervous), Weird songs (when excited)

Slug (food for bat)

Lettuce (food for slug)

Live bat

Hair: Too deep.

None of your business

Brain: Math that underlies the workings of the universe

Who's asking?

Hair: Too wide

Heart: love for sisters, love for slug

toothpick

REALLY none of your business

GERTRUDE
12 3/4 Years Old

DEE-DEE
11? possibly 27? possibly infinity?

EUGENIA
12 1/8 Years Old

Go away

Look closely at them, please. Memorize their names and attributes. They are the heroes of the book, and their names will be invoked constantly. If you don't know them, things will quickly descend into chaos.

Gertrude. Eugenia. Dee-Dee.

These three gnarly nerds did not belong at Mrs. Wintermacher's School of Etiquette; nor did they belong with their fake aunt and uncle Parquette, who had adopted them as infants; nor did they belong in the pristine town of Antiquarium; nor even did they belong in the year 1911—which is a shame because, try as one might, one cannot change the year.

Though they were not technically, biologically, sisters, Mrs. Wintermacher hated them all equally. This was because they were all equally disinterested in etiquette, instead preferring various scientific pursuits. **Eugenia** liked explosions and searching for expensive rocks. **Dee-Dee** liked building machines. And **Gertrude** was interested in things like bugs and beetles and what makes the purple feathers on pigeons sparkle and what makes soap bubbles have rainbows in them and where does a newt lay eggs and do cat whiskers feel anything and are guinea pigs related to pigs and how is a chili pepper hot and things like that.

So instead of paying attention during lessons such as "Proper Pinky Angles for Picking Up Teacups" and "The History of Soup Spoons," the Porches were usually huddled in a corner, absorbed in something else.

For instance, at that moment, Eugenia was chipping away at a rock to see if it contained diamonds, Dee-Dee was adjusting the spring tension on a miniature catapult she'd built, and Gertrude was petting the live bat stashed in her pocket.

"Dee-Dee, that catapult rules!" Gertrude whispered. "What's it for?"

"You know what they say: A catapult never reveals its destiny until the time is right," Dee-Dee said.

"Can you use it to fling me out of here?" Eugenia grumbled. "I can feel the dust settling on my brain from disuse."

Gertrude smiled at her sisters. "Too true, Eugenius."

"Now!" Mrs. Wintermacher barked. "Who would like to demonstrate for the class?" Her gentlest smile looked like the frozen scream of the weasel on her hat.

She looked out over the faces of her perfect pupils, who were all politely raising their pinkies: Imogen Crant the glue heiress; Ellabelle Belle-Parker the ballerina; Posey Picard, whose face was the inspiration for a line of under-eye creams for adolescent girls—and of course, the Porches' seven cousins, who were all perfect, and who were all named Lavinia: Lavinia-Anne, Lavinia-Vanessa, Lavinia-Jennifer, Lavinia, Lavinia-Lavinia, Lavinia-Gwyndoline—and the youngest, Lavinia-Steve, whose allergies made her one degree closer to the human experience.

Mrs. Wintermacher's gaze drifted past their raised pinkies and settled...in the corner.

"Miss Gertrude Porch," she said. "Please demonstrate."

If you'll remember, Gertrude was busy petting the bat

in her pocket—so much so that she didn't hear Mrs. Wintermacher say her name.

"Are you hungry, my good man?" she whispered to the bat.

"Excuse me, Gert-RUDE!" said Mrs. Wintermacher. "Why are you talking to your pocket?"

"Sorry, just, um, asking if it likes being part of a dress, I guess? Anyway, here I come! Make way, part the sea!" Gertrude gently squeezed her way to the front of the room, sweating in her white Taffetteen dress.

"Why does she have to be sooooo weird?" whispered Lorilyn Jennings.

"Yeah, like, a certain amount of weird is cool—" said Posey Picard, "like how I randomly twirl my hair and say 'money money money'—but she is beyond the legal limit."

"I know," whispered Imogen Crant. "She's such a MILLICENT QUIBB!"

A hush fell over the room.

"Girls!" Mrs. Wintermacher bellowed. "We do not say that name! There are no mad scientists in this town, but if there were, they would be evil, but there aren't, so shut up!"

Gertrude was used to being called a Millicent Quibb, among other things, like Slug Lover (which was true; she loved slugs), Mayor Lover (also true; she was a great admirer of Mayor Majestina DeWeen, but who wasn't?), and Most

Likely to Sweat Through Taffetteen (*definitely* true). In fact, "a Millicent Quibb" was one of the nicest things Imogen Crant had ever called her, so Gertrude took it as a win and continued journeying toward the front of the room.

Though this journey was usually accompanied by a sense of dread, but today, Gertrude was actually excited to demonstrate, for today, Gertrude had...a plan!

She had come up with a rather ingenious way to sit with a perfectly straight spine. Finally, she would do something right, and she would make her little sisters proud, and she would make her cousins like her, and she would show Mrs. Wintermacher that she could be good at etiquette and could one day be a good citizen, helping the people and animals of Antiquarium like Mayor Majestina DeWeen! Today was the day!

"Phew," Gertrude said, having finally arrived at the front of the room. "That was a long journey. I should have taken a camel up here!"

"Enough, Miss Porch. Humor is for the ugly. Now, please demonstrate the Upright Sit with Straight Back. This is the simplest of the fainting couch postures, ladies. If you can't master this, there's no hope."

Gertrude planted her feet on the ground, sucked in her stomach, pinned back her shoulders, and waited for the verdict.

Mrs. Wintermacher held an architect's protractor to her back to determine the angle of her spine.

"Ah," she said, surveying the protractor. "Out of a possible ninety degrees, Miss Porch has managed...thirty-nine. Despite her best efforts, her posture still resembles that of a dead fern."

The Lavinias snickered in unison.

Gertrude shrugged her shoulders and laughed with them, which she was very good at doing, but she couldn't help but notice that the inside of her chest felt like a bunch of dead ferns.

Eugenia and Dee-Dee didn't know what to do to help their sister, so they started clapping—which did in fact make it worse.[2]

But Gertrude pressed on. *Fear not, old chap!* she thought to herself. *For today, you have a plan!*

Gertrude faced her classmates. "Gosh," she said. "My darn spine. Bent again. What ever will I do? Oh, I know!"

Gertrude pulled a vest from her pocket, onto which she had sewn a dog's leash with a small harness attached to the end. From her other pocket she pulled a small brown bat, which she clipped into the harness.

---

2 Have you ever heard the sound of only two people clapping? It is somehow much worse than the sound of zero people clapping.

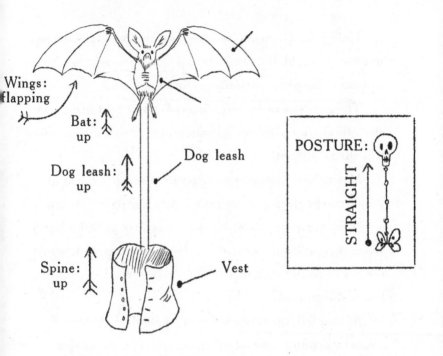

Wings: flapping

Bat: up

Dog leash: up

Dog leash

Spine: up

Vest

POSTURE:

STRAIGHT

"Behold...the Bat Straightener!"

Gertrude let the bat loose and it flew toward the ceiling, tugging on the vest and instantly improving her posture. "Ta-da! A straight spine in no time!"

The reaction in the classroom was not what Gertrude had anticipated.

Her classmates jumped back in disgust.

"Euch! The devil!" Mrs. Wintermacher screamed. She disappeared behind a heavy velvet curtain and reemerged brandishing a rusted, medieval javelin, then rushed toward the bat, poised to kill.

Horrified, Gertrude released the bat from its harness, hoping it would fly away through an open window, but instead it flapped frantically around the room.

The girls screamed and scattered. Some huddled under chenille chaises, while others attempted to pelt the bat with tiny throw pillows.

Meanwhile, Eugenia shook her head as she watched Mrs. Wintermacher zigzag around the room, waving her javelin.

"Oh, grow up, it's just a bat!" Eugenia pulled a heavy velvet curtain from a nearby window, then dragged it across the room and hurled it over Mrs. Wintermacher, tackling her to the ground.

As they fell, they knocked over a porcelain shepherdess, a vase of peonies, several Lavinias, and a lit candelabra.

"I guess velvet really *is* a cruel mistress," said Eugenia.

The flame from the candelabra spread—first up a curtain, then down a rope, then across a settee, then down a doily, then across a rug, and then up another velvet curtain, across the ceiling, and into a wooden chandelier, which came crashing down in a torrent of fire.

Dee-Dee sat quietly on the floor amidst the chaos and chewed on her toothpick, waiting for instructions. Lately she found that if she sat with her ears open, she could hear helpful whispers from the objects around her. She heard a whisper from above, where a water pipe ran along the length of the ceiling. "Break me," it said. She looked down at her miniature catapult and gave the water pipe a thumbs-up. "I see," she said to the catapult. "You have revealed your destiny."

She launched the rock that Eugenia had been chipping at, and it punctured the pipe. Just a few drops of water trickled from the crack at first, then the pipe cracked apart and a biblical flood rained down, dousing the flames.

All was still, save for the rain, and the bat fluttering out the window.

Mrs. Wintermacher punched her way out of the pile of wet velvet, smoothed what was left of her eyebrows, plucked a singed feather from her hat, and said:

"May I see the Porches in my office, please?"

"You three are officially expelled!" Mrs. Wintermacher cried.

"Ugh, fine by me!" Eugenia said. "This school is a factory of insidious conformism!"

Gertrude felt again that her chest was full of dead ferns, and that the dead ferns were now on fire. Still, she managed to raise her finger politely. "Um, Mrs. Wintermacher, the thing is, we kind of already got kicked out of the eight other etiquette schools in town, and I think our mother and father, well, our fake aunt and fake uncle, I mean, our semi-permanent adoptive mother-faunt and father-funcle, well, I think when they hear this news they might kick us out of the house—"

"That's none of my concern," said Mrs. Wintermacher. "You must face the music."

"If you tell us what direction the music is coming from," said Dee-Dee, "then we can face it and listen to it."

"It is a metaphor, you imbecile!"

Unbothered, Dee-Dee turned her head toward the southwest corner of the room. "Ah yes, I think I hear the music now. It's lovely, thank you."

"Gahh!" Mrs. Wintermacher said. "Enough! I pray that I never have to see your horrible faces again, even on a wanted poster! Now, run away before I find my javelin!"

And so the Porches sprinted to the backpack room and collected their backpacks, never to return—or so they thought.

Hot white sun baked the sidewalk outside Mrs. Wintermacher's school as the Porches trudged home.

Gertrude felt as if her guts had fallen out of her body and were being eaten slowly by pigeons and beetles. Her spine drooped even lower than thirty-nine degrees. It was all her fault.

"I'm…sorry I got us kicked out, guys. I thought the Bat Straightener was a good idea."

"This town wouldn't know a good idea if it bit it in the eyeball," Eugenia said. "We are drowning in an intellectual and moral cesspool."

"Ah, the cesspool. The humblest of pools," Dee-Dee sighed wistfully.

"I hope I can make it up to you someday," Gertrude said.

"If you can't make me thirty-six and living in Paris, then you can't do a thing for me," said Eugenia.

"I'd like some doll clothes," said Dee-Dee. "In case I ever shrink."

Though her sisters were being kind, Gertrude still felt rotten.

She wanted, more than anything, to be good, or at the very least, good enough; to be a beloved family member, an esteemed community member, a protector to all living creatures, no matter how helpless or reviled. But what it meant to be good enough in Antiquarium had very little overlap with the skills and qualities she naturally had on offer. What to do when you can't change the world, and you can't change yourself? One does grow weary, shimmying endlessly between a rock and a hard place.

Never again, Gert! she thought to herself. *From now on, keep your head down and don't do anything weird. You have to take care of your sisters....Darn, there are those tears again. I wonder what makes tears? Is it fluid from the brain? Is there a separate tear reservoir? Maybe it's in the chin, and that's why the chin trembles.*

She reached into her backpack for an old rag to wipe her face, and that's where she found it:

...the thing that would start their journey...

...the thing that would keep them up at night, forever...

...the thing that would ruin their lives, or save them, or wasn't it sometimes both?

THE MYSTERIOUS INVITATION:

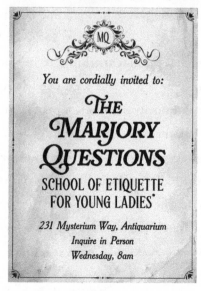

You are cordially invited to:

THE MARJORY QUESTIONS

SCHOOL OF ETIQUETTE FOR YOUNG LADIES*

231 Mysterium Way, Antiquarium
Inquire in Person
Wednesday, 8am

CHAPTER 2

MYSTERIUM WAY

MY PERFECT READER: Have you ever had a sneaking suspicion, the kind that smells of burnt toast and danger and makes your stomach drop into your feet and makes your nostrils flare like a rabbit that hears a trapper's footsteps?[1]

---

1   I know I have. I was once at the beach—that was my first mistake. Anyway, I planned to walk up a cliff of jagged rocks covered in wet seaweed. On the first rock, my sandals fell off and left me shoeless. What was I to do? I wanted to get to the top. I found a pair of dead horseshoe crabs and thought, *These would make good sandals if I tied them to the bottoms of my feet.* That's when I had my nagging suspicion: *This is a bad idea.* But then I tucked the nagging suspicion away. And what happened then? Long story short, those crabs weren't dead. They ate my toes, I fell in the water, the crabs told their friends, and now I'm being stalked by crabs. But that is beyond the scope of this book.

Gertrude Porch felt one such suspicion, upon reading her mysterious invitation.

She turned to her sisters. "Hey, guys? Is there anything mysterious in your backpacks? An invitation, or something like that?"

Eugenia and Dee-Dee riffled through their backpacks and found identical mysterious invitations.

"What is this?" Eugenia asked, looking over the invitation. "Who on our green earth is Marjory Questions, and why does her name have an asterisk?"

"Let me ask," said Dee-Dee. She whispered gently to her invitation, then held it to her ear. "The invitation doesn't want to say; it has a headache."

Gertrude thought hard about the source of her sneaking suspicion. Yes, there were the asterisks, but there was something else...something more trenchant...a smell... yes, smell, the sense most potently tied to memory...yes, a smell, from her early childhood...where had she smelled that smell before?

She racked her brain. Was it the time Aunt Desdemona brought home leftovers from an Italian restaurant? Was it the time the cook made ketchup soup? Or was it the time she found...

the note in the sand?

When Gertrude was seven, she'd gone on a beach out-
ing with the Parquette family. She'd been brought along
specifically to carry the towels, but still, it was an honor
to be invited! She unwrapped sandwiches for the Lavinias, unfolded a heavy chair for Uncle Ansel, and set up a
giant umbrella for Grantie Lettuce, who was Aunt Desd-
mona's ninety-eight-year-old grandmother. Then finally,
after everyone had gone off to stand in the water, Gertrude
found herself sitting alone with Aunt Desdemona, and
mustered the courage to ask about the things that were not
supposed to be asked about.

"Um, Aunt D? What was my mother like?"

Aunt Desdemona froze. "She was...you know. She was
neat. I didn't really know her that well."

"Well, wasn't she your best friend?"

Aunt Desdemona was unusually pale. "Yes, right, of
course. Like I've told you a thousand times, she was my best
friend. Your mother and Eugenia's mother and Dee-Dee's
mother. All of us, best friends, until their tragic group
death."

"Yes, but...what were their names?" Gertrude asked.

"Um...Pookie."

"All of them?"

"Yes. The Pookies. They lived on a...farm. It was a...
garlic farm."

It seemed to Gertrude that Aunt Desdemona was improvising instead of recounting. "Whoa. So, um, what happened to them?"

Aunt Desdemona's eyes darted around the beach, as if she might find the answer printed on the back of someone's umbrella. "They died. Of...garlic. They were struck in the head during a garlic avalanche. Tragic. My best friends. There, are you satisfied?"

Gertrude was not really satisfied. Her only memory of life before the Parquette family was a single grainy flash of being in a cold room full of cribs—but that couldn't be right, and anyway, all she really wanted to know was...had a grown-up ever held her and been happy about it? Had she ever filled someone's heart with joy? Had she ever been 'home'? If it was so, she wanted to remember it, so that she could feel it, even for a second.

Just then, Gertrude noticed something odd at her feet: the graceful shell of a moon snail, with a little scroll of paper rolled inside. The scroll read, in microscopic calligraphy:

I'll be watching you
When the time is nigh
Mad science is real
And so am I
—Millicent Quibb

Gertrude gasped. Who would write such a blasphemous note?

She tucked the note back into the shell, unsure of what to do next, but Uncle Ansel immediately chucked it into the ocean. "Rude-Gert! Don't! Touch! Disgusting! Snails!"

Grantie Lettuce wagged a single creped finger: "Don't be a Silly Sally."[2]

After that, Gertrude tried hard to forget about the note, but she could never forget the way it smelled...

faintly of tomato sauce.

Eugenia flicked Gertrude on the shoulder, pulling her from her reverie. "You look like you've smelled a fart," said Eugenia. "Is there a problem?"

"No, it's not that, it's...Well, remember that note I found on the beach? From you-know-who? Well, it sounds weird, but this invitation kind of smells like that."

Eugenia hung her head. "Ugh. That was a prank. Millicent Quibb isn't real—she's a story they told us to keep us from wearing pants."

"I know. Just made me think of it is all."

The three puzzled together in the sun.

---

2 Who is Sally? Why is she silly? These, and other questions, are beyond the scope of this book.

"I think this is a sign," said Dee-Dee.

"Um, a sign of what?" asked Gertrude.

"To stop."

And Gertrude and Eugenia glanced upward to see that Dee-Dee was in fact pointing to a stop sign.

Eugenia slung her rock-filled backpack over her shoulder. "We'll deal with these random invitations later. For now, we have…

"Gertrude, Eugenia, Dee-Dee…how do I say this delicately…? We're considering giving you away."

The Parquette family was dining on their daily supper. At one end of the grand dining table sat Aunt Desdemona and Uncle Ansel, calmly slicing away at their rabbit loins. Next to them sat Grantie Lettuce, who was sipping pureed rabbit through a straw. Along the sides of the table sat the seven identical Lavinias, and in their laps sat seven identical bichon frises,[3] distinguishable only by the color of the bows in their hair.

---

3 The bichon frise, a white poof, is the official dog of Antiquarium, and by "official dog" I mean "the only legal dog," according to the *Town Codes of Antiquarium*, Section 900.4F.

At the other end of the table sat the Porch Sisters.

"I'm sorry," said Aunt Desdemona, "but this latest incident is the final nail in the camel's coffin. We have tried to keep you, out of a sense of duty and piety. But I don't see how we can continue—now that you are convicted arsonists."

Gertrude coughed. "Yes, Aunt D, I understand. Accidental arson is arson nevertheless—"

"You three committed the ultimate violence!" Uncle Ansel wept. "You destroyed *furniture*! How could you be so cruel as to destroy innocent couches?"

Grantie Lettuce's gray head creaked from side to side. "I smell a Silly Sally."

Lavinia-Anne smoothed the white silken hair of her panting bichon frise. "I'm afraid of them, Mommy."

"I know, my darling. Hush now."

"You're completely right, Aunt D," said Gertrude, trying to keep her voice from quivering. "I really bit the big one, but I *promise* it will never happen again. Next time I swear I'm going to stay on the straight and narrow, behavior-wise! I'll study, I'll be polite, I'll be normal...."

"There will be no next time," Uncle Ansel cried through a mouthful of rabbit. "There is no other school in Antiquarium that will have you! You've been ejected from all of them! You must go!"

"So...you're kicking us to the curb?"

"Unfortunately, no. We cannot have you embarrassing us by walking the streets, so we have found you all a placement at an etiquette school..." Aunt Desdemona said, pausing to dab the corners of her mouth with a napkin, "...in Austria."

Gertrude panicked and stood from her chair. "But it was all my fault! Just send me, please. I don't care what happens to me, I just want Eugie and Dee-Dee to be all right. Don't punish them for my mess-up!"

Eugenia stood with her sister. "If she goes, we all go. I'm dying to live in Europe anyway! We'll make cuckoo clocks! We'll see the Alps!"

"I've always wanted to meet an Alp," said Dee-Dee.

"There will be no cuckoo clocks, nor Alps," said Aunt Desdemona. "It is an institute called Die Versagenschule, which means "The School for Failures." It is for girls who cannot be corrected by conventional means. There are a lot of Doberman pinschers there—but not in a fun way."

Gertrude pictured herself in a prison yard in Austria being chased by Doberman pinschers—but not in a fun way.

"We've already arranged for your boat ticket," Aunt Desdemona continued. "You'll leave in the morning. Go now and pack your backpacks."

Gertrude's heart thrummed. All was lost. Her innocent sisters were going to be mauled by Doberman pinschers, and it was all her fault, and now she had to go pack her backpack, and...wait! Eureka! Of course! Backpack! The mysterious invitations—perhaps they didn't have to go to Austria after all!

"WAIT!" she yelled, darting from the table. She zoomed to her backpack and, thinking fast, pulled out the mysterious invitation, then hurtled back to the table and shoved the invitation in Aunt Desdemona's face. "Look! We actually already got invited to another etiquette school, right here in town!"

Aunt Desdemona peered at the gold cursive. "The Marjory Questions* School of Etiquette for Young Ladies*? Is this one new? It sounds fake."

"Um, well, no, it's actually extremely real!" Gertrude said, though she wasn't entirely convinced herself. "It's... state of the art, it has a giant pool of soup, and if you eat with the wrong spoon they push you in, and you boil...? We were basically invited...um, on scholarship."

Aunt Desdemona's ears perked up. "Scholarship, you say?" Aunt Desdemona looked to Grantie Lettuce, who nodded her crusty gray head, then she began again. "I must admit, Gertrude, I am intrigued. The School for Failures is *extraordinarily* expensive, and we do not want to pay for something that probably won't work if there is still a free option. So that settles it. You'll go tomorrow."

That night, the Porches lay awake in their bedroom, which was behind the main house. Well, behind a *pond* behind the main house. Well, a pond and a tennis court. Well, a pond and a tennis court and a wood chipper and a compost heap. Yes, behind all those things was the Porches' bedroom. It was a shed made of rotting wood, but the sisters loved it more than anything because it was their own, and they could pursue their hobbies without scrutiny. Gertrude ran a playground for slugs and a hospital for crickets and a school for baby birds out of some of the Lavinias' used dollhouses. Eugenia kept a collection of gems with which to furnish her future Parisian apartment and a collection of powdered chemicals to mix into explosives. Dee-Dee had rigged the whole room with a machine that could pull back the roof at night so they could see the stars, and on her bedside table sat a piece of banister that she claimed sang her lullabies—who were the others to say any different?

"I wonder if Marjory Questions will have a welding torch," Dee-Dee mused.

"At an etiquette school? Dream on, Doo-Dee," Eugenia said, hammering away at a chunk of granite. "We are about to be buried once again by boredom, like our mothers in garlic."

Dee-Dee gazed wistfully at the stars overhead. "Gertie, tell us about the garlic farm again?"

And Gertrude, the oldest sister, keeper of the earliest memories, recounted her usual details about the garlic farm: the size of the garlics, the Pookies making shrimp scampi, how the Pookies loved all of them very much. All from imagination, of course—because her real memory about the sterile room of cribs was just not very pleasant, and who doesn't want to make life better for one's little sisters?

Later, while Eugenia and Dee-Dee slept, Gertrude lay awake with her favorite pet, a slug named Salvatore, as he made lazy figure eights on her forehead.

"Sal?" she whispered. "Do you think there's any place for us? Me and Eugie and Dee-Dee? Any place on this earth?"

Gertrude crossed her eyes to check in with Sal, who had stopped on her nose. But Sal had no answers. He curled up like a kitten on the pillow next to her and fell into slumber—and in time, so did she.

"You three will have to walk today," Uncle Ansel said without looking up from his morning paper. "I'm bringing the Lavinias in the car because it's two whole blocks and their feet hurt."

And so the Porches set out on foot with their backpacks and their lunch boxes, following the route they'd marked in red on an old map of Antiquarium. They walked past the firehouse and the butcher, past the church and the other church, past the town fountain. Eugenia huffed, Dee-Dee hummed, and Gertrude sang to pass the time:

Taffetteen, Taffetteen

The itchiest fabric that there's ever been.

By the time they reached the cemetery on the outskirts of town, the children were drenched in Taffetteen sweat. They'd never been so far from the center of town, and were surprised by how dingy and dead everything looked.

"Is it too late to go to Austria?" murmured Eugenia.

The Porches trawled up the outside of the cemetery, which was lined with ivy and barbed wire. Across the street was a gated archway draped with thorny brown vines. A painted sign on the gate read:

Mysterium Way

They looked both ways as they crossed the street, even though the only living thing for miles was a murder of crows mewling miserably overhead.

"This is not right," said Eugenia. "If this is an etiquette school, then I am a cheese danish."

"Interesting. I've always thought of you as more of a croissant," said Dee-Dee.

Gertrude couldn't help but agree with Eugenia, but her feet wouldn't listen. She told them to bolt away, back to the comfort of home, but instead they inched forward, almost oozing, farther and farther down the dark cul-de-sac.

The derelict houses of Mysterium Way were each missing something important—one lacked walls; another, a roof; and another was just a cereal box nestled amongst a bushel of reeds.

"I think you're right, Eugenia," Gertrude whispered. "This is definitely weird. Maybe we should leave?"

Suddenly, the weather turned, and the children found themselves standing in the middle of a dark May thunderstorm. They squinted as they stared up at the house at the end of the cul-de-sac.

Number 231 was a decrepit mansion five stories high, with a looming tower. Sections of the roof had been burned away. Gray wallpaper rattled in the wind like ashen newsprint in a dying fire. Hot rain pelted the open rooms. Lightning cracked, sizzling a crow as it flew past.

Gertrude stared at the front door, which was covered, inexplicably, in barnacles.

A gust of wind blew a branch of blackened holly away from the mailbox, revealing the sign that hung beneath,

Millicent Quibb's House

Door: covered in barncales (why?!)

Sign made of moths! (with special choreography!)

FLOOR PLAN

Fire flea observatory — 4th floor elevation

Bathroom (with colony of giant mussels) — 3rd floor elevation

Laundry room / Gemistry lab — 2nd floor elevation

Observatory (for observing chicken of the sea—NOT tuna)

Pastramibird apiary

GROUNDS

Gazebo

House

Electric roses (CAUTION: 10,000 volts)

Powder room (full of unidentified powder— DO NOT ENTER)

Greenhouse roof

a sign made of shimmering brown material, with letters in red:

THE MARJORY QUESTIONS
SCHOOL OF ETIQUETTE FOR YOUNG LADIES

As the girls peered closer, they could see that the sign was actually made of hundreds of moths. Suddenly, with a flutter of the moths' wings, the colors of the sign rearranged themselves, revealing a new sign altogether:

THE MILLICENT QUIBB
SCHOOL OF ETIQUETTE FOR YOUNG LADIES
OF MAD SCIENCE

"I knew it!" Gertrude cried. She grabbed her sisters and turned to run, but by then it was too late.

For there, standing before them, was a lady...

....no, a creature...

.....a harbinger of doom...

......a person with very crazy hair...

.......the myth, the legend, the fact...

MILLICENT QUIBB

CHAPTER 3

ORIENTATION

MILLICENT STARED AT the children.

The children stared at Millicent.

Her hair was a chaotic nest of salty, windswept fibers, thick as sea rope, that were somehow black and gray and colorless all at the same time. She stood six feet tall—five, if you didn't count the soles of her boots. Her lab coat was of charcoal wool and tailored in the manner of a scout's uniform. It was splattered with stains of all colors and textures—a neon green smear, a dribble of oatmeal, a matrix of dried intestines. Her face was neither kind nor mean but pulsating with life and purpose. She was not, in any case, as terrifying as the nursery rhyme indicated—until she opened her mouth.

"Ahhhh!" Millicent cackled. "My trap worked. I've got you cornered! And now I'm going to pickle your brains! AHHHAHAHAAAAHAHA!"

The jaws of the Porch Sisters flew open as they set to screaming. Eugenia screamed! Gertrude screamed! Even Dee-Dee, who had never screamed before, pulled the toothpick from her mouth and gave it a whirl!

"Oh no! I was kidding!" Millicent cried. "You know the rhyme the children sing about me? About how I pickle brains? I feel insecure about it, so sometimes I turn it into a joke! Please stop screaming—you're making me nervous!"

The children did not stop screaming. Their screams rattled the windows of the crumbling mansion, rustled the ivy on the entrance of the cul-de-sac, shook the tombstones in the cemetery across the street.

"Oh dear, Antonio—I think I've scared them!" Millicent said.

The Porches looked around for the person that Millicent Quibb might be talking to—a hunchbacked assistant, say, or hulking enforcer—but the truth was far more heinous. She was consulting with a small blue hermit crab in the palm of her hand.

"Antonio, I think the school might be off to a bad start! What do I do?"

The hermit crab waved one of his tiny blue claws, as if to say, "I've never done this before, I don't know."

"Well, they're just sort of standing here and screaming, so, do you suppose you should round them up and get them inside?"

The hermit crab sighed and wiped his brow, then emerged from his shell.

Suddenly the Porches remembered that they had feet, and began to run away.

"No! Don't go!" Millicent cried. "The orientation! I bought bagels! Antonio, hurry!"

The hermit crab scuttled toward the fleeing children, unspooling himself from his shell like a kite. When most hermit crabs emerge from their shell, they reveal only a little nubbin of guts—this one seemed to have an impressive length of soft blue intestines, which unfurled endlessly from his shell like a magician's trick. The crab twirled in quick circles around the fleeing feet of the Porch Sisters, until finally the girls fell to the ground in a heap, their ankles bound by crab intestines.

"Good work, Antonio!" said Millicent Quibb. "Now can you do something about the screaming? I don't want to attract attention!"

Antonio nodded, then scuttled across the girls' Taffetteen shoulder pads and pinched each of their earlobes in a way that made them fall instantly asleep.

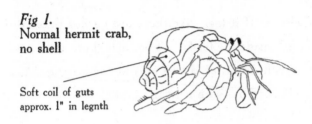

Fig 1.
Normal hermit crab,
no shell

Soft coil of guts
approx. 1" in legnth

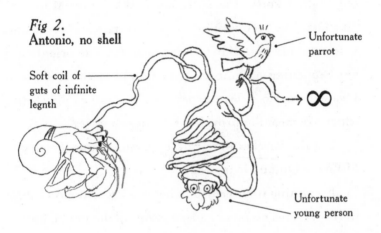

Fig 2.
Antonio, no shell

Soft coil of
guts of infinite
legnth

Unfortunate
parrot

Unfortunate
young person

"Well! Thank goodness we got them!" said Millicent. "It's a crime to waste a bagel!"

When they came to, the children found themselves sitting on chairs that were, for lack of a better word, alive.

"This is my living room. Do you like it? Don't mind

the chairs. If it feels like there are guinea pigs squirming around inside the backs, it's because there are."

Eugenia sputtered like an old car engine. "Y-y-you—you—lassoed us—with a hermit crab!"

"Did I?"

"YES!"

"Ugh, I know, I'm sorry about that," said Millicent. "It's just, I've been waiting so long to start my school and it seemed like you didn't understand that the orientation was happening *inside* the house instead of on the street, and I wanted you to at least experience the guinea pig chairs, which are meant to provide a relaxing massage."

But the Porches were finding it impossible to relax in Millicent Quibb's living room.

Everything in it seemed to be moving, and most things were. A cactus bloomed, a fern crept up the wall, a leather credenza breathed. The shelves were lined with jars of sick-yellow and jaundice-auburn liquid, with fetal pigs and purple frogs and fish intestines floating inside; a lizard that bore the exact markings of the wallpaper behind it; a lizard reading a miniature book; a lizard that had a carrot for a tail—anything in the world could be found pickled in jars on Millicent's bookshelves. No surface was uncovered by dust or dried roots or crawling chameleons. The chaos of it made the children squirm—to say nothing of the guinea pig chairs on which they sat.

"Egggggsellent," Millicent began. "Now. I've never started a school before, so I'm just as nervous as you are, probably more so!" This was incorrect, as the Porches were scared for their very lives, but Millicent did indeed look nervous.

She cleared her throat as she adjusted her collar, then read from her clipboard. "Hello. This is your orientation for the Millicent Quibb School of Etiquette for Young Ladies of Mad Science. I am Millicent Quibb."

Dee-Dee nodded approvingly, wanting to provide emotional support through Millicent Quibb during what was obviously a difficulty with public speaking.

"Now, I wrote down a list of things to ask the pupils, if the pupils actually showed up, so the first item is: What is your experience with mad science?"

The Porches could only stare silently with their mouths open.

"Alright, I'll put 'none.' Now, if you have no experience with *mad* science, can you tell me about your regular scientific interests?"

Their jaws remained frozen, until Gertrude managed to whisper: "Are you...really *her*?"

"Yes, I am she. The very same."

"Enough of this…psychological torture!" Eugenia said, her usual sarcasm tempered by a sudden shortness of breath. "Why don't you just…pickle our brains and get it over with!"

"Nonsense!" Millicent said, clutching the lapels of her lab coat. "I would never pickle a human brain!" The children each heaved a sigh of relief. "They're too bitter, you have to *candy* them."

Their collective sigh turned into another collective scream.

"Shhh! Please, there is no screaming at this school. Now: you must have *some* scientific inclinations…do any of you like…plants? Bats? Rain?" Millicent tapped her fingers impatiently. "What are your *passions*, dears? You must live a life animated by passions or you will perish, as a shark who ceases to swim drifts listlessly to the ocean floor and begins to rot. So. Tell me your passions, and from there I can determine your mad science disciplines.[1] You there—your passions?" Millicent flicked a long pointer at Eugenia's nose.

---

1 For a list of these, please see Appendix A in the back of the book. But do return to this page afterward! Mark the page with your finger, an envelope that had a doctor's bill in it, a flower—I don't care, but do return!

"I suppose, if threatened, which I am, I would say that I like rocks."

"Ah, wonderful. We'll put you down for **Gemistry**."

Millicent flicked her pointer at Dee-Dee. "You, with the toothpick. Your passion?"

Dee-Dee calmly pulled the toothpick from her mouth. "It is machines, sir."

"Ah, thank goodness!" Millicent said. "You can fix my refrigerator. I'll mark you as a **Fryzzicist**. Eggsaladent."

"Excuse me, madam," Gertrude whispered, "did you mean to say, um, 'excellent'?"

"No, I meant to say 'eggsaladent.' It is similar to 'excellent' but with more mayonnaise." Millicent turned to Gertrude. "Speaking of, my dear Gertrude: What are *your* interests?"

Gertrude had plenty of interests: She wanted to open a hotel for injured camels; she wanted to join the cabinet of Mayor Majestina DeWeen as Secretary of Insects' Rights; she wanted to invent a protective suit for slugs so that none would die of salt. But no one had ever responded to her dreams with anything other than groans and taunts, so she'd learned to keep them a secret.

"I...don't know?"

Millicent's eyes rolled back until they were completely white. "You DON'T KNOW?" She cocked her head to the left and peered at Gertrude. "I would venture to guess that underneath all that ridiculous Taffetteen, you have a strong instinct for **Unnaturalism**, the study of unnatural creatures. That's the field of mad science that I practice. I have spent my life finding, researching, and caring for these creatures."

This might have sounded wonderful to Gertrude, were she not so worried about her brain being candied.

Millicent turned away from the sisters and looked out the window. "The truth, ladies, is that I did not need to ask about your passions. I already knew them."

"Then why did we waste those precious ten minutes?" Eugenia said.

"Um, ma'am, if I may," said Gertrude, "how do you know our passions?"

"I have been watching you."

"I knew it," Dee-Dee said with a nod.

I'll be watching you

When the time is nigh...

"The moon snail...," Gertrude whispered. "Was that actually...you?"

Millicent looked around the room frantically, as if searching for someone else, then pointed quizzically to herself. "Who, me? Ah, yes, I used to leave those on the beach as pranks to frighten children. I certainly haven't been watching you for your entire lives or anything like that, that would be weird. Anyway, now that we've done the intake, let's move into the laboratory so that I can give you your uniforms!"

This was all moving very fast, and Gertrude was feeling lightheaded. "Um, ma'am, before we go, can I just talk to my sisters first?"

Millicent began to dust a jar of eyeballs with her skirt. "Pretend I'm not here."

The children leaned across the arms of their guinea pig massage chairs and whispered amongst themselves.

"So, we're all in agreement that she's gonna kill us?" said Eugenia. "On three—run. One...two—"

"The hermit crab is guarding the door," said Dee-Dee. Indeed, Antonio had unspooled himself and woven a thick web of hermit crab intestine over the entire doorframe. "But that window over there is telling me that it's unguarded." Dee-Dee nodded to an open window past the dining table, which housed a colony of popping prairie dogs.

Gertrude looked at the escape window, then back at Millicent. "Yeah, I guess we should leave," she whispered.

Millicent sighed dramatically. "Alright. I understand. You are free to go." She placed her eyeball jar back on the shelf. "Yes, I was eavesdropping. Look—I know I'm 'scary' and my house is 'a hoard' and there are 'tarantulas everywhere.' I'm not 'good with children' and I don't 'have social skills.' I was 'kicked out of etiquette school when I was young' and now I'm 'a pariah.' So go—go back to your etiquette schools, where they will turn you into the sorts of mindless, Taffetteen-shrouded lemmings who contort themselves to fit into the impossible templates set by this ridiculous town. I'm sure you will all make fine lemmings. Goodbye."

"It's not you, it's us," Eugenia said, ushering Dee-Dee and Gertrude toward the dining room. "Thank you so much for the guinea pig massage. Bye-bye."

"THE TOWN IS IN DANGER!" Millicent blurted suddenly, raising her arms to the sky. "Listen to me well, children, and mark my words: There are bad actors in this town!"

Eugenia rolled her eyes. "Yes, we know, we all saw the Antiquarium Players' production of *The Tempest*."

"No, not *those* kind of bad actors. There are people in this town who seek to harm! I fear that evil forces are being awakened, forces that have been dormant for centuries, forces that could destroy us all! But together we could stop them! If you want to help the people and animals of this town, then you must join me!"

Gertrude stood still, even as Eugenia tugged on her arm. She knew that all she wanted in the world was to help people and animals.

"Accompany me on *one* mad science expedition," Millicent pleaded, "and I will show you the real history of this town, so that we may rescue its future. If you are bored, we will part ways, no hard feelings. Just *one* expedition." She sunk to her knees. "Don't you wish to know the truth? DON'T YOU HAVE A SENSE OF ZINUS?"[2]

"What on earth's hot crust is 'Zinus'?" Eugenia spat.

"Zinus is a...a tingle in the spine, a sense of adventure, a sense that something is about to happen. ZINUS!"

Eugenia folded her arms across her puffed-up chest. "NO! I do not have a sense of Zinus, I have a sense that you're preying on our good natures in order to eat us! Therefore, good day!"

Eugenia dragged Dee-Dee to the open window in the dining room. "Gertrude! Come!"

Oh boy, Gertrude thought. *What do I do? If Aunt D and Uncle A saw me right now, in Millicent Quibb's living room, they'd probably bonk me over the head with a frying pan and leave me in the desert to be eaten by hyenas, and Eugie and Dee-Dee would get shipped off to Austria, and my life as I know it would be over forever, and it would be my fault. Then again...when I think of helping people and animals, I do feel a sense of, I guess, ZINUS?*

---

2 "Zinus" (pronounced "ZY-niss") is a broad term that can mean 1) a sense of adventure; 2) the joy of life; 3) the color in the universe; 4) the smell that is sometimes on your earring backs when you take them out of your ears.

Hmmm...this one sure is a humdinger. What is a humdinger, anyway? Is it a kind of bird? Sounds like either a bird or a bug—

Eugenia hoisted Dee-Dee onto the windowsill. "Gertrude! Why aren't you coming?!"

Gertrude tried to walk toward her sisters, but then... the strangest thing happened. Her feet stopped working. For the second time that day, she felt like they were melting. She almost toppled over. Something would not let her feet leave Millicent Quibb's house.

"Okay, Miss Quibb," said Gertrude.

"ONE EXPEDITION."

CHAPTER 4

THE EXPEDITION

I'M SO GLAD you decided of your own free will to accompany me on just one expedition."

Millicent marched proudly down Main Street while her reluctant new pupils followed behind.

"I will now show you the real story of this town, and why I believe it is in danger. Come, let us perrrrrrambulate under our *parrrrrrapluies!*" said Millicent Quibb in a high-pitched trill.

"Why are you talking like that?" Eugenia snapped.

"To blend in, my dear! I am a master of disguise!" said Millicent. But it was hard to blend in the presence of Millicent Quibb, even in what she'd referred to as her "normal person disguise": a poofy dress in the shape of a yellow cupcake, with a sun hat so wide that it knocked into other hats as they walked.

"Now: we begin our expedition here on Main Street!" she warbled. "A bustling thoroughfare, home to regular old candy shops and shoe stores and ice cream cones. Rrrrrright? Wrrrrrrrong!" Then she turned to the children and lowered her voice to a whisper. "Did you know that our fair town of Antiquarium used to be the Capital of Mad Science of the Northern Hemisphere?"

The children looked quizzically at the cobblestone street underfoot. They were surrounded by the flapping of doves, the quiet fluttering of butterflies, and the passing of parasols. There was nothing particularly, shall we say, *mad science-y* about it.

"Not to patronize, ma'am, but I think you may be confused," Eugenia said.

"About most things, yes, but about this, no! You see, one hundred fifty years ago, this town was *crawling* with mad scientists. Yes, the hamlet that we call Antiquarium was a beacon, a vanguard, a touchstone. As New York is to finance and Paris is to cheese, so Antiquarium was to the magnificent art of mad science! You couldn't walk two feet without stepping into a laboratory or a repository or a tunnel or a trapdoor!"

There was a sudden gust of unseasonably icy wind, to which Dee-Dee tipped her hat.

"Then why haven't we seen any of these things?" Eugenia demanded.

"They are all buried, of course. After the Great Fire of 1761, they simply built another town on top, a town where mad science was outlawed. Come, I shall prove it to you."

As they marched on, the children whispered nervously amongst themselves.

"I can't believe you volunteered us for this eight-course tasting menu of delusions," Eugenia said, elbowing Gertrude in the ribs. "Mad science is a fiction. She is just an animal hoarder with a florid imagination and some good party tricks."

Gertrude had to admit that it might be true. The only truly inexplicable thing she'd seen thus far was the incredible length of Antonio the Hermit Crab, who was now asleep in Millicent's pocket—but who was to say that he wasn't just an exotic species with a particularly long tail?

"Maybe," Gertrude said, "but what if she's right, and the town *is* in trouble? Dee-Dee, what do you think?"

"I don't know," Dee-Dee said, "but I do know that I did not appreciate what some of her windows were telling me. They were saying that my destiny is to be a sea captain. I don't know how I feel about that. I'd be a very short sea captain."

Gertrude and Eugenia just nodded. As strange as

Dee-Dee was, the things she said were usually, in some manner, true.

"Now: these shops may look regular," Millicent continued, pointing to the window of a candy shop. "But did you know that this store used to be a boutique called Budget Corpses, which sold body parts for viological experiments? 'Buy an arm and a leg without paying an arm and a leg' was their slogan."

"Fascinating," Eugenia said, rolling her eyes.

The farther they marched, the more outlandish Millicent's claims grew. In front of the furniture store: "This used to be a school for unnaturalist zookeepers." The pickle shop: "This was a gemistry lab where they turned split peas into emeralds." The toy store: "A fryzzics emporium that sold vacuum cleaners powered by black holes." The town swimming pool: "Used to be a pond for Beanburp Birds. I wouldn't swim in there if you paid me."

Still, none of them were convinced.

Suddenly, Millicent stopped at the stone steps of the bank, where a chip about the size of a piece of pie was missing from the steps. "And at last we have arrived at the Danger portion of the expedition. Exhibit A: the broken steps. *This* appeared several days ago." She bent down to investigate the minor damage with a magnifying glass and jotted something in her notebook.

"This is what we're looking for," Millicent said. "Keep your eyes peeled for more signs of trouble."

Eugenia's eyes hurt from rolling.

Millicent noted other aberrations as they passed. A missing brick from the facade of a building: "See?!" A hairline fracture in the sidewalk: "Aha! Danger afoot!" A streetlamp bent slightly to the side: "Ooooooh, mama, this is bad!"

And indeed, the Porches had never seen even such minor blemishes on the normally perfect and pristine face of the town of Antiquarium—but none of these seemed cause for alarm.

"Miss, um, Quibb?" Gertrude said. "Can I ask what you think this, um, danger may be? The danger you keep talking about?"

"Well, I do not know for certain, Gertrude my dear," she said. "But I do harbor a sneaking suspicion that a certain ancient evil has been stirring and...AHHHH!"

Millicent screamed as though someone had torn off both her legs, though it was unclear just why.

They were standing in front of a fountain in the town square, a fountain with a tall marble statue in the center. The statue depicted Antiquarium's first mayor, Jacobus DeWeen, and bichon frise, Amanda, venerated throughout history for her brilliant mind, kind nature, and stylish ponytail. But today, the ponytail that usually plumed from

Before
(with ponytail)

After
(NO PONYTAIL!)

Mayor Jacobus DeWeen and
his beloved bichon frise
AMANDA

the top of Amanda's head was somehow cruelly and inexplicably...missing.

"Horrors! I was right! My Tinglies™ were trying to warn me! I should always listen to my Tinglies™! I thought I might be overreacting, but I was right!"

"What are you right about?" Gertrude cried.

"It's true!"

"What's true?" Gertrude cried.

"They've returned!"

"Who've returned?"

Millicent sank to her knees and cried to the heavens.

"THE KRENETICS RESEARCH ASSOCIATION!"

Passersby stared at the woman in the neon Taffetteen.

Gertrude tapped Millicent on the shoulder and whispered, trying to get her to quiet down on the busy street: "Um...Madam, er, Teacher Quibb, what actually is the Karmetics Rehearse Proclamation, or...what did you just say?"

"The Krenetics Research Association!" Millicent said incredulously. "The KRA! Have they taught you nothing in school?"

"Honestly, no," said Gertrude.

"Well then, I must start at zero," she said, pulling the children into an alleyway behind a dumpster. "Listen closely. The KRA was a sinister cohort of evil mad scientists. It was in the Heyday of Mad Science, before the Great Fire of 1761, when they went about their foul work. They stopped at nothing in their quest for power, money, and eternal life! They stole, they maimed, they killed! They were monsters making monsters, terrorists making terror, rubes making ruses, and now...THEY HAVE RETURNED!"

Eugenia put her head in her hands. "I'm sorry. You think we are at the mercy of an ancient cult because...a *dog's ponytail* has gone missing?"

"*Exactly*," Millicent said. "On Sunday I saw the trouble—the cracks in the concrete, the broken stairs, the missing bricks—and I knew in my bones that something was wrong—and this missing dog ponytail proves it! That is why I chose this moment to start my school. I cannot fight them by myself! I must pass on my knowledge to a new generation, in the event of my death, so that the KRA does not win!"

"So you want *us*, a group of children with no skills at all, to help you protect the town against a hidden organization of evil mad scientists?"

"*Yes*. You're finally getting it."

"Well, you can get some other kids to do it," Eugenia said. "We're busy."

"But...please!" pleaded Millicent. "It must be you! You are special. All of you!"

Gertrude was interested to know in what way she might be special, because no one had ever called her that—at least, not in a good way—but Millicent was probably just trying to trap them in some sort of brain-candying operation...right?

"I know this missing dog ponytail doesn't seem like a big deal, but trust me: The Squevil is in the details.[1] Come.

---

1 A Squevil is a type of ant that buries itself inside the details of lace curtains. The Squevils themselves are harmless, but you must ask yourself why they are there, for if you do, you'll find that the Squevil's natural predator, the Frith Rat, is sick. And when a Frith Rat is sick, you need to get out of your house, because they happen to fart carbon monoxide. The point is, everything is interconnected, and when some small thing is out of balance, typically there is a bigger problem somewhere else. A problem that may prove...deadly.

Let us find out what happened to this statue. If we find no evidence of foul play, I'll let you go back to your lives as before, and I shan't call upon you agayne."

Suddenly, a crowd of reporters and photographers and bystanders closed in on the fountain. The flashbulbs crackled like fire as a shining figure approached the statue. Millicent and the Porches ran to the other side of the fountain and ducked. Gertrude peered over the lip of the fountain and, to her shock, saw that the shining figure was none other than...

...the resplendent...

...the amazing...

....the legendary...

MAYOR MAJESTINA DEWEEN

Gertrude felt compelled to curtsey. Majestina DeWeen stood six feet tall. The dramatic arches of her black eyebrows seemed to move independently of the rest of her face. She was a part-time jazz singer and full-time politician. Her voice was brassy, her manner dulcet; she could sing like an angel and belt like the devil. She was, in a word, fabulous.

Gertrude poked her sisters and said in a scream-whisper: "THAT IS MAJESTINA DEWEEN!"

Gertrude wanted to call out to the mayor. "Hello, I am

Gertrude Porch!" she would say. "I want to be in your cabinet so I can help people and animals, like you!" But instead she just waited behind the statue and tried not to breathe too loudly.

The cameras and reporters gathered around the mayor as she began a public address. "This morning, tragedy has struck our quaint town of Antiquarium. Last night, someone defaced the statue of my beloved ancestor Jacobus DeWeen, removing the ponytail of his beloved bichon, Amanda. Of course we all know that Amanda DeWeen was a remarkable creature. She was a genius and a saint. She could do math with her paws, she barked full sonnets, and she once cured a man of typhoid after he combed her beatific ponytail. Only a villain would mar her memory in such a disturbing fashion."

Majestina's secretary of finance, the lawyer Ashley Cookie, Esq., handed her a tissue from his side bag. "I don't need that, male Ashley. Now: I encourage all citizens to remain cautious until we can apprehend the vandal who destroyed this hallowed symbol of civic pride. Thank you."

The crowd applauded wildly as Majestina and Ashley Cookie, Esq., marched away in a solemn procession.

Gertrude wished she could follow the mayor all the way back to the Town Hall of Antiquarium to share her ideas about insects' rights, water conservation, and rabbit health—but Millicent had other plans.

"Come!" she whispered to the children. "We must look for clues!"

Millicent and the Porches followed a hairline crack in the pavement, over the sidewalk, across the street, around the corner, and down Cobblestone Alley, which was, as you could maybe guess, a cobblestone alley.

Dee-Dee ran like a gazelle, Eugenia felt that this was all a horrible waste of time, and Gertrude—well, in between worrying about what would happen if the Parquettes were to spot them, Gertrude allowed herself to feel a small sense of what could only be described as *ZINUS*.

Just then, Gertrude came to a sudden halt. She noticed something in a shadowy corner of Cobblestone Alley.

A hole.

But it wasn't just any hole: Its circumference bore a distinctive pattern, a pattern that looked almost like...teeth.

"Um, Madam Quibb?" Gertrude asked. "I might have found something?"

Millicent fell to her knees on the cobblestones. Her eyes were wild. Frantically she leafed through a book in the shape of a small cube—tiny, but thick—that she had pulled from a pocket in the folds of her aggressively yellow skirt. Gertrude peered at the title: *The Encyclopedia of Monstrous Bites.*

Bite? Gertrude pondered. *This is a cobblestone street! What kind of animal takes bites out of cobblestone streets?*

Millicent peered back and forth between the book and the circle, book and circle, book and circle.

"I can't believe it," she said finally. "All these years I've been searching, waiting, standing vigil. And here it is. My Tinglies™ were right, as was my sense of Zinus, and this proves it. This is…this is…"

And then Millicent said, just before collapsing to the ground:

"THIS IS A KYRGALOPS HOLE!"

Fig 1. Kyrgalops bite pattern

Fig 2. Kyrgalops mouth

Lips

Teeth
(can crunch
through diamond)

More teeth

8 ft wide when fully grown

So many teeth

So sharp!

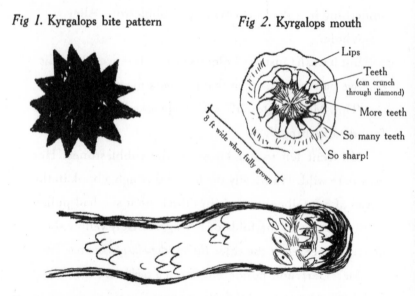

Encyclopedia of Monstrous Bites. Page 679.
The Kyrgalops (CUR-ga-lops): A giant worm that can eat through stone. Extremely dangerous.
Invented in 1632, bred by the Krenetics Research Association in Antiquarium, currently extinct.

CHAPTER 5

A TRIP TO THE LIBRARY

BUT YOU STILL haven't said, um…what does it mean…that there is a Kyrgalops hole? And what is a Kyrgalops?"

Gertrude and her sisters ran breathlessly after Millicent, who charged through the streets of Antiquarium—to where, she would not say.

"A Kyrgalops is a worm!" Millicent cried, darting down an alley. "A monstrous worm with giant teeth that can bite through stone—a worm that is supposed to be extinct! It was always illegal to breed a Kyrgalops, even in the heyday, but guess which evil organization was crazy enough to do it…?

THE KRAY"

"I have to go to the bathroom," said Eugenia.

Millicent shook her head. "*That's* what you have to say right now?"

"Yes, and public toilets are a no-go for me."

"Then hold it. We must verify that what we've seen is in fact a Kyrgalops hole. And so we must find out more about the Kyrgalops, a creature about which I know very little."

Gertrude gulped. "And, um, where will we find out, Mrs. Quibb—?"

"I answer to MS. Quibb, Professor Quibb, Doctor Quibb, Demon-Lizard Quibb, anything but 'Mrs. Quibb'!"

"Okay, um, Demon-Lizard Quibb, where will we find out?"

"Where does anyone find anything out?

AT THE LIBRARY, OF COURSE!"

The Porches followed Millicent in her neon yellow Taffetteen up Wellman's Hill and over Sickman's Bridge and down the bank, where the canal met the reedy swamp.

"This is not, as I have been saying for the past forty-five minutes, the correct way to the library," said Eugenia.

"There is a leech on my shoe. I never get leeches on my shoe when I'm going to the library."

"It's not that kind of library," Millicent said, smiling slyly. She grabbed her wrinkled lab coat from her handbag and pulled it on over her dress. "Ah, much better."

The lab coat pooled around her waist as she waded farther into the reeds. She approached a single, tubular flower: long and white, with a stem that curled into something resembling a French horn.

"Mad Science Etiquette: Lesson one," Millicent said. She pulled a leather folio from her coat pocket and riffled through a thousand loose papers. "Where oh where oh BEAR is that chart? Ah! Here it is!" She handed the children a stained purple mimeographed worksheet.

Gertrude furrowed her brow at the worksheet. It was wonderfully interesting—the amazing flowers, their amazing attributes, their amazing appetites—but the farther they waded into the reeds, the more she felt the safe tedium of their former lives slipping away. She wondered whether perhaps they'd be better off on a boat to Austria, and whether perhaps she had led her little sisters astray yet again with her big ideas.

"This is the Hornflower. See on your diagram? We need to entertain the Hornflower with a last-minute light lunch so that it will let us into the library. Whatever will we serve?"

Carnivorous Plants of Antiquarium
Millicent Quibb School—Lesson 1

Hornflower

Diet:
1. Voles / moles
2. Rhino meat
3. Mac and cheese
4. Annelids

Kissing Tulips
(CAUTION—
DO NOT KISS)

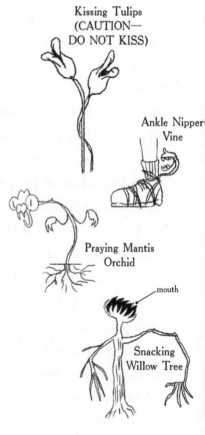

Ankle Nipper
Vine

Praying Mantis
Orchid

mouth

Snacking
Willow Tree

Tongue-leaf Plant
(Hides under piles of leaves—
RAKE YOUR LEAVES!)

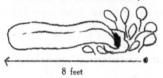

8 feet

The Porches read the list of items enjoyed by Hornflowers. "Rhino meat?" Eugenia whined. "Where are we
supposed to get rhino meat?"

Dee-Dee's legs were tired, and she thought that this was as good a place as any to sit down and chew on her toothpick.

Gertrude scanned her memory. There were no rhinos in this suburban marsh, no voles, no moles, no mac and cheese, and as for annelids...EUREKA!

"Um, Ms. Quibb? I think that, um, actually, annelids are segmented worms?" she began. "I know 'cause I once had an earthworm that I named Anne Lid so I could remember the family name for worms,[1] even though she really looked like more of a Stephanie—"

"Get to the point, dear."

"Anyway, I believe that leeches are actually also a type of segmented worm? So, can we feed the flower a leech?"

Millicent smiled like a cat with a secret. "Good, Gertrude."

Good? Gertrude frowned. Whenever Gertrude answered in class, she was met with yelling or snickering—never had she been met with a simple "good." She decided that this was probably mockery, even though Millicent Quibb did seem pleased.

"Now, gather leeches while ye may, children."

The Porches dipped their hands below the muck and

---

1 Please see Appendix B for a family tree of the Wonderful Worm Family

pulled some slimy leeches from their shoes, then handed them to Millicent.

"Watch closely now, this is something one ought to know how to do." The Porches looked on nervously while Millicent lifted a handful of leeches to the mouth of the Hornflower. They screamed with a mixture of horror and delight as the Hornflower scarfed down the leeches.[2]

Suddenly the Hornflower blew a low note, a note that trembled the reeds and made the mud quake beneath their feet. The reeds parted, and the top of a marble staircase emerged from the muck, a staircase that led down into the darkness.

Gertrude felt instantly dizzy. She looked to Eugenia and Dee-Dee, who were feeling the same. There it was: Proof! Incontrovertible proof! There was not a flower on earth that could eat that many leeches, then blow a note that opened a secret staircase in the middle of a swamp, according to the laws of plain science. The Hornflower had to be one of the...what did Millicent call them? Unnatural creatures? Which begged the question: Were there *other* unnatural creatures? How many different kinds? How

---

2 Nota bene: When feeding a Hornflower, make sure the palm is FLAT! Human fingers are easily mistaken for leeches. If you see a Whatanist* walking around with a stump where a finger ought to be, you could bet that she forgot to KEEP THE PALM FLAT.

*Breeder of Unnatural plants.

would you care for them in a menagerie setting?

"Here, at last, is the library...," said Millicent. "The Mad Science Library of Antiquarium."

"I'm not going down there," said Eugenia.

"That's fine," said Millicent. "You can stay up here with the hungry leeches."

Dee-Dee placed a gentle hand on Eugenia's chest. "The stairs want us to come," she whispered. "It would be rude not to."

Eugenia knew that when Dee-Dee deigned to speak, it was best to listen.

And so it was that the Porches started down the staircase, slipping on the marshy marble and skirting snakes as they descended into...

THE DEEP.

"Here, let's take a map," said Millicent, plucking an ancient pamphlet from the abandoned welcome desk. The pamphlet promptly disintegrated into dust.

"I see," she mumbled. "No one has updated the pamphlets since 1761. I do that every time I come here, I don't know why I never learn. Anyway, we need to get to the Viology wing, which I believe is...this way?"

Gertrude surveyed the foyer, a gleaming marble hall three stories high with soaring arches. This place had once been grand, meaning that someone had once thought mad science was worthy of things like marble staircases and soaring arches—maybe even a lot of someones!

A word burbled into Gertrude's brain—from where, she did not know.

The word?

Zinus.

This is amazing! Mad science is real and I feel a sense of Ziiiiinusssss...!

She wanted to sing, as she did when she was excited, but she kept it to a low whisper song.

The children followed Millicent down a dark hallway illuminated only by dim blue blobs that bobbed through the air.

Gertrude paused to marvel at a glowing orb and, without thinking, reached up to touch it.

"I wouldn't touch the floating jellyfish, dear," said Millicent.

"Is it because they sting?"

"No," she replied. "It's because they *explode*, and the guts eat your hair and then make a hole in your skull and then the *other* jellyfish eat your brain through the hole with straws. But close. Anyway, careful!"

Eugenia shook her head. "How has my short life come to this?"

The hallway was lined with heavy wooden doors covered in metal spikes. Each door bore a placard of increasingly worrisome designation.

AMBULATORY POTATOES

ETERNAL BUBBLES

DENTAL PEOPLE

"Who are the Dental People?" whispered Dee-Dee.

"People made out of teeth," said Millicent. "I wouldn't go in there. They have NO sense of humor."

Eugenia, who could maintain skepticism about the existence of fists even while being punched in the face, took a deep breath and opened a door labeled INVISIBLE ROCKS. Inside was nothing but blackness.

"Ha. See? A hoax." She walked into the room and then howled in agony as she conked her forehead on something invisible above, then stubbed her toe on something invisible below. "Owwwww! What was that?"

"Oh dear. Should I have stopped you from walking into the invisible rocks?" Millicent asked. "I don't know about children. Are you supposed to stop them from hurting themselves when they're being ignorant or are you supposed to let them do it so they really learn?" She sighed. "Eh, tell me later."

While no one was looking, Eugenia wrestled a small chunk of invisible rock from the monolith inside the room and put it in her pocket.

As the group reached the end of the hallway, they paused under a tattered banner that read VIOLOGY.

Gertrude wondered if it was a typo, but if so, it was an awfully large one. "So did they mean 'biology' or—?"

"Absolutely not," said Millicent. "*Viology* is another matter entirely. You see, where Unnaturalism is the discovery of the unnatural creatures that already walk among us, Viologists invent new creatures, using surgery and other unsavory methods. I have never...actually visited this wing of the library. I find it distasteful."

"So these footprints belong to someone *else*?" Dee-Dee asked. She pointed with her toothpick at a set of fresh footprints that disappeared into the Viology wing.

Millicent froze. "No," she whispered. "No no no no no. SOMEONE HAS BEEN HERE ALREADY!"

"But I thought you were the only mad scientist in Antiquarium!" Gertrude said, shaking.

"So did I," Millicent said gravely. "Follow me."

The four shuddered as they tiptoed through the hall of Viology, which was lined with dimly lit dioramas of increasingly unpleasant taxidermied creatures: a giant saber-toothed frog; a shark with a snake for a tongue, with a cockroach for a tongue, and with an ant for a tongue;[3] and finally, behind a vast wall of glass, the Kyrgalops: a long red worm, four feet in diameter, covered in gleaming crimson scales sharp as daggers, with four tiny feet and four crossed eyes. But the most horrifying thing was the mouth: a fearsome round maw lined all the way around with crunching teeth made of thick rocks.

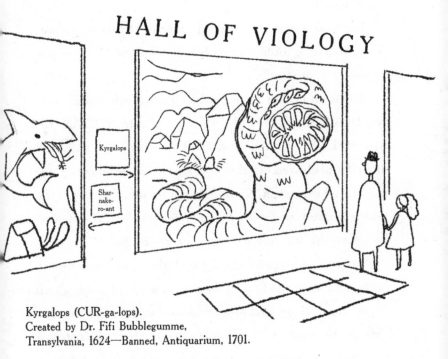

HALL OF VIOLOGY

Kyrgalops

Shar-
nake-
ro-ant

Kyrgalops (CUR-ga-lops).
Created by Dr. Fifi Bubblegumme,
Transylvania, 1624—Banned, Antiquarium, 1701.

3 The dreaded Shar-nake-ro-ant, one of the grossest creatures ever dreamt up by
the human brain, in my opinion.

"Hello, friend," Dee-Dee said, tipping her cowboy hat. "*Enchanté.*"

The group scanned the display for anything out of the ordinary, other than the horror of the creature itself. Near the back of the worm, by its four little feet, was a nest made of jagged shards of granite. In the nest were three egg-like orbs, red as rubies, and an indentation where a fourth might have been.

Gertrude gasped and tugged softly on Millicent's sleeve. "Um, Madam Quibb, doesn't it seem like one of the eggs is maybe, um, missing?"

Millicent peered through the glass and screamed, "OH NO GOOD GOURD PLEASE NO THIS IS A DISASTER ALL IS LOST WE ARE DOOMED!" Then she collected herself and cleared her throat. "Yes, I can see where an egg may have been taken. Good eye, Gertrude. Of course the oddness here is that none of the glass is broken. If someone has taken the egg, how did they breach the glass?"

Eugenia, who privately enjoyed glass and happened to know a lot about it—being that glass is made of sand, which is just crushed-up rocks—scanned the window for defects. "Hmm. Interesting. Not that I care, but there is a patch of glass that has a different refractory pattern from the rest. Again, not that I care. But look here—"

Eugenia poked the tinted circle of glass with her finger and was shocked to discover that her FINGER WENT RIGHT THROUGH IT.

Millicent threw her glasses to the ground.

"I knew it!" she shouted. "Jellyglass! How dreadful. Do you know what you have to murder in order to make Jellyglass? Ten kittens. Oh dear. I shouldn't have said so. I see Gertrude is doubled over in emotional pain—"

But Gertrude wasn't in pain—she was trying to get a better view of the back of the diorama. She had spied something inside the display, on the ground—something that didn't belong. A feather—a long, thin, purple feather shaped like a question mark. But the Kyrgalops was a featherless creature, as far as she could see. What was a feather doing inside there, and why did it look familiar to her?

She scanned her memory. Was it in a book about weird feathers? Was it on a pigeon that needed a haircut? Was it on a dog playing dress-up?

Suddenly, she knew.

"That feather...I've seen it before...there was one just like it...on one of..."

"Get to it!" Millicent cried.

"On one of...

MRS. WINTERMACHER'S HATS!"

ENTR'ACTE 1

HERE I FEEL we need a short break. You have done so much reading already, and I'm proud of you. I personally hate reading, unless it's an instruction manual. I relax with manuals in the tub at the end of a long day. Last night I was so entranced by a manual on toaster repair that I fell asleep in the tub. I still look like a shar-pei.

Anyway, though this whole book is technically an instruction manual for the young mad scientist, you've certainly done a lot of reading of "scenes" and "story"—historically accurate though they may be—you've yawned at "characters" and "dialogue"; valiantly you've drudged through the interminable muck of "description" and "themes." All of these are things I personally find too tedious to bear, so I wanted to provide you with a reprieve that is STRICTLY INFORMATIONAL. Please enjoy.

MAD SCIENCE ACTIVITY:

HOW TO THROW A WEB USING A FUNNEL CAKE SPIDER:[1]

1) Lay one Funnel Cake Spider on a flat surface and scratch its back with dollhouse-sized back scratcher. Spider should roll over and purr like a cat.

2) Remove back scratcher. Spider will become irate and will look at you like, "Excuse me, what happened to the scratcher?"

3) At peak irateness, poke the abdomen (gently, of course). Spider will release a web. The web will float away like tiny soap bubble, with rainbows cascading across the surface.

---

1 Available by mail-order catalog from Suleiman's Mobile Spider Emporium, current address unknown.

4) Blow web (gently, of course) to desired location.

5) Wait for web to settle and expand. Final result will resemble a carnival funnel cake.

WARNING:
DO NOT EAT WEB.[2]

I hope you feel refreshed, inspired, and enlightened. When you are ready to climb back into the story, remember that Gertrude, Eugenia, and Dee-Dee have just learned that the town bogeywoman, Millicent Quibb, is real, and there is some kind of rock-eating monster on the loose, and their former etiquette teacher may have something to do with it. What will they do next?

LET'S WATCH!
I MEAN. READ!

---

2 Just...don't. Trust me. Your eyebrows will explode, and that will be the least of your problems.

CHAPTER 6

SPY SNAIL

SO. YOU HAVE COME to beg my forgiveness."
Mrs. Wintermacher sat smugly in her leather office chair.

"Yes, Mrs. Wintermacher," Eugenia said through a
plastered, clownish smile. "We realize how much we took
this majestic institution for granted! We love you now!"

"I always loved you!" said Gertrude.

Dee-Dee merely smiled and fidgeted in her chair, as
she was the one holding the Spy Snail inside her Taffetteen
overcoat.

Oh dear.

My darlingest reader—my pleasant, intelligent, perhaps
redheaded reader, fine if you're not—I have dropped in a
detail that I should have explained before the chapter started.

Let us rewind fifteen minutes, to when the Porches were sitting in Millicent's car, which was idling outside Mrs. Wintermacher's school. They were trying to hide themselves from view, which was difficult in Millicent's car because it is a Gerbilcar, and though a Gerbilcar may look like a regular car, it is in fact powered by hundreds of gerbils on wheels, and it sounds and smells as such.

"Great getaway car," Eugenia said. "It blends right in."

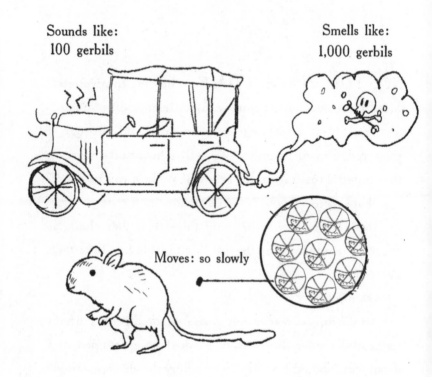

Sounds like:
100 gerbils

Smells like:
1,000 gerbils

Moves: so slowly

Millicent ignored Eugenia's famous sarcasm and reached into a secret compartment beneath her feet. "Today's mad science etiquette lesson is this: When you suspect foul play, you must be the final snail in the coffin."

Eugenia sighed. "Don't you mean 'final *nail* in the coffin'?"

"No. I do not misspeak. Please stop insinuating that I do. I said *snail*." And from the compartment she pulled a moist snail about the size of a football helmet. "This, my pupils, is a Spy Snail. His name is Lou."

Though Gertrude liked the look of Lou the snail, who reminded her of her own beloved Salvatore the slug, she was feeling overwhelmed and wondering if maybe there was a difference between having fun looking for holes in an alleyway and engaging in dangerous subterfuge with living equipment.

"Clearly," said Millicent, "your former headmistress is somehow involved in the stealing of the Kyrgalops egg. What she is up to, we do not know. Thus, we need to gather evidence. Lou will serve as your eyes and ears. If you wear the shell as a helmet, you can see and hear everything that he sees and hears. His antennae can extend up to three feet and are thin enough to fit through a keyhole in a trunk."

"Wow," Gertrude whispered reverently. "How will Lou get inside?"

"Oh, you'll bring him in. You'll ask to be reinstated in the school, and then you'll hide in a trunk and spy on Mrs. Wintermacher."

"What if there is no trunk?" Gertrude asked.

"It is a headmistress's office," Millicent said. "Rest assured, there will be a trunk."[1]

Eugenia shook her head. "No. Not happening."

But one learned quickly that with Millicent Quibb, things you thought weren't happening were already very much underway.

And that is how the Porch sisters found themselves groveling in the office of Mrs. Wintermacher, just a day after having been expelled.

"We have come to, um, beg of your sweet mercy, Mrs. Wintermacher," said Gertrude.

Mrs. Wintermacher twirled a sharp letter opener on the tip of her finger, as though contemplating murder.

"Do you see this portrait of me, children? I just had this painted."

---

1 "All headmistresses offices must contain at least one big, heavy trunk." *Town Codes of Antiquarium*, section 5.98B.

Behind her hung a grand oil portrait in the classical style, depicting Mrs. Wintermacher on horseback, in traditional ladies' hunting costume, surrounded by hounds, teeth bared. (Both hers and the hounds').

"Did you know that I grew up in squalor? Yes, I lived in a tiny log cabin in the Swiss Alps with my jolly old grandfather. 'We don't have much,' he always said, 'but we have one another! And isn't that grand?'"

She stabbed the letter opener into the surface of the desk. "Well, I didn't think so! I didn't want pigeon guts for dinner, thank you very much. So I stole all his money and ran away to Frankfurt on my thirteenth birthday, where I became the leader of a gang of pickpockets.

"We were the toughest crew in the city. We started laundering the money through an etiquette school. Eventually I got sick of the life and opened my own chain of etiquette schools. Sold it for three million in '89, and here I am today."

She sighed contentedly. "So you see, my little nerds, today I am the headmistress of a school of etiquette. But tomorrow...I will be so much more. Because Ursula Wintermacher gets *everything*."

Gertrude cast a sideways glance at Dee-Dee and Eugenia. Was Mrs. Wintermacher...all right?

"Sure, come back to my school. It doesn't matter. Big things are underway, so the point is moot. I will go get your reinstatement forms. You three can scamper on back to class, but please stop at the nurse's office on your way for a power-hosing and a de-licing. Gourd knows where you three have been."

Mrs. Wintermacher clomped out of the office and let the door slam behind her.

Instead of wandering off to the nurse's office for a power-hosing, the Porches opened the trunk under Mrs. Wintermacher's window[2] and climbed inside.

Gertrude strapped the Spy Snail to the top of her head, her heart thudding so hard that it rattled the trunk. *I am the mayor of Anxiety City*, she thought. *I swore I would try to not draw attention to myself anymore and try to keep my sisters safe—and now I'm wearing a snail and spying on Mrs. Wintermacher? Maybe I was just hallucinating that the feather was from her hat. Am I hallucinating now? Oh, help me!*

Lou's snail eyes wended their way through the keyhole of the trunk, and suddenly Gertrude could see and hear everything in the office.

It was her job to wear the snail, because she was the most comfortable in the intimate presence of slimy creatures.

It was Dee-Dee's job to spray perfume to cover up the smell of Lou, a smell which could best be described as "old yogurt in a hot car."

---

2 See? All headmistresses have trunks!

It was Eugenia's job to keep feeding Lou little bits of a chocolate bar. "Lou is soothed by chocolate," Millicent had said. "If he doesn't get his chocolate, he will make a sound. You'll know the sound when you hear it. You don't want him to make the sound." Eugenia had rolled her eyes, but she didn't want Mrs. Wintermacher to hear the sound, whatever it was.

A moment later, Gertrude watched as Mrs. Wintermacher returned to her office, reinstatement forms in hand. She tossed the forms onto her desk, then opened a drawer below. Then, to Gertrude's surprise, Mrs. Wintermacher pulled out a large piece of granite.

"Snuggles, my priceless angel...are you ready for your snack? Mummy has your snack!"

Mrs. Wintermacher stood on her tiptoes and unhooked the gargantuan hunting portrait, then set it on the ground.

Behind the oil portrait, cordoned off by steel bars, was a rectangular hole in the wall, about the size of a fireplace—and behind that was a dark void.

Suddenly, a creature emerged from the blackness—an enormous worm covered in sharp red scales, with four eyes and a round mouth lined with a circle of thick stone teeth, teeth that turned and gnashed like the stone gears of a prehistoric clock. Gertrude knew it instantly.

"It's a Kyrgalops!" Gertrude whispered. "She has a Kyrgalops!"

Gertrude felt instantly that her body was made of loose pudding. It was easy to imagine that Mrs. Wintermacher, the woman who had tortured them with napkin-folding lessons and salad-eating contests, was perhaps a wearer of fur coats or an eater of veal—but never did it cross their minds that she might secretly be a dangerous mad science outlaw.

Mrs. Wintermacher managed to shove the heavy rock through the bars of the Kyrgalops cage. The worm gnashed at the granite and pulverized it in an instant with its grinding teeth.

"Good boy, Snuggles! Soon, my darling, when you are big enough, you will serve your purpose. You will live out your destiny, and I will live out mine!"

Just then, the phone rang.

"Mrs. Wintermacher's School of Etiquette for Girls, how may I direct your call?" she said. She looked around to make sure no one was listening, then began again. "Yes, 'tis I....Yes, the worm has been contained....There was minor damage, a few bricks, a bent lamppost, and the unfortunate matter of the de-ponytailed marble dog....Yes, the cage has been reinforced, but the worm is ravenous, and it can eat through the bars....I have been feeding it a granite block every fifteen minutes to keep it sated—I've barely slept." She sighed, trying in vain to wrestle her desk lamp away from Snuggles. "But rest assured, I will contain the beast until Sunday, when it will reach full size, whereupon I will lure the worm to the desired location, and we will be off to the races!"

Gertrude stiffened. Today was Wednesday, which was very close to Sunday. What was Mrs. Wintermacher planning to do with the worm on Sunday?

"Thank you for checking in," said Mrs. Wintermacher. Then she pressed the back of her hand to her forehead in a kind of salute. On her palm was a somewhat shoddy tattoo, a red circle with three letters in the center:

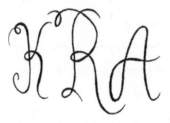

"In the name of our gracious leader, Talon Sharktūth— may he reign forever!"

Mrs. Wintermacher hung up the phone, sank back into her leather chair, and sighed a contented sigh. "Ursula Wintermacher, you brilliant woman," she said to herself, kicking her feet up on her desk.

And that, my friends, is when the Porches ran out of chocolate.

Eugenia fumbled through the mess of foil wrappers looking for chocolate, any chocolate—a square, a shard, even a smear—but found none. "I'm all out of snail snacks!" she hissed.

Gertrude pulled Lou the Snail from her head and bounced him in her lap, hoping that might soothe him. He jerked his snail head this way and that, searching every corner of the trunk for chocolate, poking the children with his wandering googly eyes. Then, unable to find even a morsel, the snail began... **TO WHINE.**

And oh, how he whined. He whined like a boy in a candy store being told he cannot have any more gummy peaches; like a Lavinia at Christmas being told that there were no presents left to open; a wailing whine, an insistent wine, a whine so piercing that the Porches had to cover their ears to survive it.

"Who is whining?" they heard Mrs. Wintermacher say. "Snuggles? No, not Snuggles..." She clomped around the office in her steel-toed boots. The sisters clung to one another as her footfalls drew closer.

"I have loved you all," Dee-Dee said. "May our souls meet again one day for quiche."

The sisters squeezed their eyes shut and listened to

the sickening sounds of their own demise: Mrs. Winter-macher's steel-toed boots clomping toward the trunk, her fingernails wedging themselves under the lid, the metal hinges creaking open. The end, it seemed, was nigh.

Then: another sound, a miraculous sound!

"Excuse me, Madam Wintermacher?" Someone was shouting from the hallway—and the Porches had a good idea of who it might be.

"Oh, what now?" Mrs. Wintermacher grumbled, dropping the lid of the trunk like a dead fish.

"My name is Professor Alsacia McAlistair Flemingbottom. I seek a position at the school."

The girls peered out from the trunk. Mrs. Winter-macher had left the office and slammed the door behind her. From the trunk, they could hear the unmistakable vocal stylings of Millicent Quibb in the hallway.

"I owned a chain of etiquette schools in my native town of…McScotland…shire. I am known as one of the hardest disciplinarians in the business." Millicent's accent was so thick and so fake that one couldn't tell whether she was pretending to be from Scotland or Saturn.

"Hardest disciplinarian, you say?"

"Yes," Millicent replied. "I…hit the children with rocks! Yes. In the head. With small rocks."

"I see. Well, we don't do that here," Mrs. Wintermacher

said, turning back toward her office. "Much as I would like to. Good day."

Quickly, the Porches darted from the trunk and struggled to pry open the window behind Mrs. Wintermacher's desk.

"Wait! I was kidding about the rocks!" Millicent said. "In reality, I am an expert in the areas of napkin folding, harpsichord cleaning, casually glancing at watches…"

While Mrs. Wintermacher listened impatiently, the girls managed to wedge the window open, then dropped into a nearby shrub and ran for their lives!

"…eating peas one at a time, folding the hands in the lap—"

"Thank you, Professor Flemingbottom, but we already cover those areas in our curriculum, and we won't be needing help at this time."

"Shame," said Millicent, peering into the empty office. Satisfied that her pupils were gone, she spun on her heels and strutted away.

Mrs. Wintermacher hurried into her office and found everything as it was before, except for the trunk, which was now…open.

"Curious," she murmured.

She hunched over the trunk to find it empty, as usual, save for...a mess of empty chocolate wrappers and the scent of perfume. "Curiouser."

She riffled through the wrappers and found them empty, save for a few shards of chocolate and a faded sticker no bigger than a postage stamp: a label, of all things. It read:

Spy Snail™, *1908.*
Property of Millicent Quibb.

"Well, I'll be darned!" Mrs. Wintermacher said to the Kyrgalops, who had already crunched through two of the new steel bars over its pen. She hurried over and lifted another granite block to the worm's lips. "My, you are a hungry beast. There, there. Well, Snuggles, it may interest you to know that it looks like the legendary buzzkill Millicent Quibb is still alive...

BUT NOT FOR LONG."

CHAPTER 7

TBD

THE CHILDREN RAN. They ran and ran from Mrs. Wintermacher's office until they could run no more! They ran so fast that Lou the Spy Snail was carried off into the wind. They ran because there was nowhere safe to go: Millicent Quibb had sent them into a lion's den, Aunt Desdemona wanted to send them to Austria, and Mrs. Wintermacher wanted to do gourd knows what with the Kyrgalops. They ran because everything they thought they knew about Antiquarium, the starched Taffetteen collars and pink parasols and delicate dessert forks, was a lie. They ran because even the ground beneath their feet held secrets, and the sky above roiled with the dark clouds of conspiracy. And so they ran to the one place that made sense, the one place they felt safe, the one place where sanity ruled the day. They ran...to the duck pond.

MY PERFECT READER: Is there a place you go when it's all too much? When you are too overwhelmed and too frightened, and you need simple comfort?

For me, this place is a seafood restaurant.[1] For the Porch Sisters, this place was the Antiquarium duck pond: an undulating expanse of green water hugged by willow trees and populated by a batch of rowdy teenage mallards, snippy Canadian geese, and one lonely blue heron.

The sisters shivered together at the edge of the pond. "Did you know duck siblings can communicate with each other while they're still in their eggs?" Gertrude said.

"Yeah right. Do they have little phones in there?" Eugenia said.

"I'd love to live in an egg. No property taxes," Dee-Dee said.

They stared out at the water birds.

"Maybe it was all a dream?" Gertrude said. "Mrs. Wintermacher and the worm and everything?"

"Maybe we'll just never hear from Millicent Quibb again," said Eugenia.

---

1 I like cracking king crab legs with that little silver cracker; I like an entire dish of hot, wet butter; I like wearing a little bib. Okay? I like little bibs! Sue me!

"Maybe it's NOT my destiny to be a sea captain," Dee-Dee said.

And for a moment, it seemed possible that the nightmare had been just that, and all was well. The girls tried to focus on things that were the same as they'd been that morning: the sun on the water; the chirping of sparrows; the lazy length of the heron's wings as it drifted over the pond; the goose with the note card in its mouth, lumbering toward them.

Wait. That wasn't the same.

And yet, it was happening. Yes, a beady-eyed goose with a cameo choker tied gracefully around its neck was waddling in their direction, bearing a message. The goose dropped the note card in Gertrude's lap, then paddled off, honking all the while.

Gertrude's hands shook as she unfolded the note card, which smelled vaguely of tomato sauce. It said:

> *Dear Pupeels,*
>
> *Hello. I don't blame you for running. That was craaaaaaazy! Anycrab, obviously we have much work to do, namely, figuring out how to trap the Kyrgalops before Mrs. Wintermacher lures it to the desired location. There is only one man who would know about such things: the worm's original*

creator, Dr. Fifi Bubblegumme. We must make
our way to his laboratory, to locate his diary. The
journey will be a harrowing one. One or more of us
will probably perish. The entrance will be lined with
horrific creatures designed to kill on contact. Only
a mad scientist with ample training will be able
to reach the laboratory, and even then, it will be a
struggle.

Therefore, you must train. It will be grueling.
I will teach you everything you need to know in
order to battle the KRA. Your skin will harden, your
bangs will burn, your minds will be trapped in a
psychological prison of broken mirrors and strange
echoes. And at the end of it all, you'll be lean, mean,
KRA-fighting machines.

Come back tomorrow?
It's your decision.
Would you like to train
For your first mission?

—"Marjory Questions"

The Porches stared at the messenger goose as it disappeared behind a willow tree.

"Well," Eugenia said. "She said it's our decision. We
can die trying to rescue this ungrateful town, or we can go

to Austrian prison, OR—and this is what I've been advocating for all along—we can run away to Paris! We can pawn one of Uncle Ansel's cuff links and buy an apartment!"

Dee-Dee was pensive. "I would personally like to go back to Ms. Quibb's school. I wish to see the laboratory of Dr. Fifi Bubblegumme." She looked to Gertrude. "You are the oldest and the wisest. What do you think we should do?"

Gertrude was feeling very overwhelmed. She had never intended to get her sisters wrapped up in a deadly adventure with a mad scientist, and she doubted very much her ability to save them, let alone the town. She'd never succeeded before—why would this time be any different?

She wiped a tear from her eye, then pretended that she was just scratching an itch.

"Well?" Eugenia asked. "What do you think we should do?"

"Um..." Gertrude searched the pond for an answer, but none came. "My answer is...TBD!"

"TBD?!"

"Yes," she said, relieved at the temporary reprieve. "I just need a little more time for my answer to be...determined."

"How much more time?"

"Just until...after dinner!"

Dinner that night was plain buttered spaghetti, which the Parquettes strained to cut into thousands of little pieces.

"Um, could I have the salt, please?" Gertrude said.

No one moved to pass her the salt, so Gertrude just tied several strands of spaghetti at the ends to fashion a long rope, which she tossed down the table and used to lasso the saltshaker.

As she was pulling the salt toward her, Grantie Lettuce severed the rope with a swift chop of her knife.

"I smell a Silly Sally," she croaked.

But Gertrude was too caught up in the ropes of confusion to care.

An hour later, dinner was over, and she was no closer to knowing what to do.

The Parquettes settled in for their favorite evening activity, a parlor game called "Critique." The game went as follows: Lavinia-Steve (the Contestant) glided back and forth across the living room, a heavy book balanced atop her head, while the rest of the family (the Critics) sat on the couch and scrutinized her every movement through opera glasses. Each person held up a numbered scoring paddle at the end.[2]

The book would not stay perfectly flat atop Lavinia-Steve's head, because beneath her perfect blond ringlets, her skull was bumpy, and beneath her perfectly bright smile, her heart carried a secret, but that is beyond the scope of this book.

The book wobbled, and Lavinia-Steve began a chorus of tiny stress sneezes.

Aunt Desdemona sighed. "Lavinia-Steve, if you insist on sneezing like a common...sneezer, don't even bother taking a turn. Zero out of ten."

"Negative three," croaked Grantie Lettuce.

Lavinias Anne, Vanessa, Jennifer, Lavinia, Lavinia-Lavinia, and Gwyndoline snickered. "Hahaha, Lavinia-Sneeeeze!"

Gertrude looked over at her youngest cousin, barely eight years old, who was trying valiantly to laugh at being called Lavinia-Sneeze. Gertrude could relate to such things. She cast Lavinia-Steve a kind smile, and Lavinia-Steve smiled back, wiping a tear from her cheek.

I should try talking to Lavinia-Steve sometime, Gertrude thought

---

2 The game had been described as "fun for the whole family!" in a recent best-seller called *How to Break Your Child's Spirit Without Really Trying*.

to herself. *Maybe she's a little nicer than the rest of the Lavinias.* But Gertrude put the thought away for later, as she had a decision to make.

"Speaking of failure...Gertrude, how was the new school?" Aunt Desdemona asked.

Gertrude cleared her throat for too long. The truth was that the new school had almost, well, killed them. The truth was that mad science was real and Millicent Quibb was real and there was an evil cabal trying to take over the town and Mrs. Wintermacher had a rock-eating worm that she was maybe probably going to unleash on the town in a few days and everything was topsy-turvy and nothing was right and..."Good? It was good. We learned all the different kinds of...butter knives?"

"Ah, an important topic indeed," Uncle Ansel said with an approving nod. "Now, this Marjory Questions—to what school of etiquette does she subscribe? The Burbleboop Method? The Ruler-Smack Technique?"

"Oh, the...um...Hermit Crab School?"

Eugenia pinched Gertrude's knee.

"Interesting, I hadn't heard of the Hermut Krabb School," said Aunt Desdemona. "Must be German. Fair! So, the three of you will go back tomorrow? Or shall we ship you to Austria?"

Before Gertrude could answer, the family heard a

peculiar grinding sound coming from the street. They turned to look out the parlor windows to the sidewalk, which glowed under the streetlamps. Outside, Mrs. Wintermacher was dragging a boulder down the street, past the mailboxes and the picket fences, sweating and puffing and looking very nervous.

"Why is Ursula Wintermacher dragging a boulder down the street?" Aunt Desdemona asked.

Suddenly, Mrs. Wintermacher dropped her rope and ran to knock on the front door of the Parquette house! What was Mrs. Wintermacher doing? Had she come to get the Porches in even more trouble?

Uncle Ansel moved to greet her at the door. "Ursula! Is everything alright?"

"Help!" she cried. "Do you have any big rocks? Any boulders?"

"No, we haven't any boulders...," said Uncle Ansel.

"Okay, well, let me know if you find any! Goodbye!" And she hurried to the next house and rang the doorbell, muttering nervously under her breath.

"How odd!" Aunt Desdemona said. "Well, I guess she's building a stone cottage."

Grantie Lettuce pursed her lips in a barely perceptible pucker. "I smell a Silly Sally...."

Meanwhile, the Porches could only stare soberly at their

shoes. There could only be one reason that Mrs. Winter-macher was running around the town asking her neighbors for spare boulders: the Kyrgalops was getting bigger, so much bigger that granite blocks would not suffice. What-ever she was planning, no one would be spared—not her, not her sisters, and not the Parquettes.

Gertrude looked around at the deeply flawed collection of people that were the only family she'd ever known. Even though Aunt Desdemona was high-strung and Uncle Ansel was histrionic and the Lavinias were snide, none of them deserved to be maimed by a giant worm, and if the Porch Sisters could do anything about it, then it was their duty to do so.

The Parquettes settled in to continue their game of Critique. "Where were we?" Desdemona asked. "Ah yes. The Marjory Questions school. You'll return tomorrow?"

Gertrude steeled herself and sat up straight, knowing that the right thing and the hard thing were often the same thing. She smiled nervously and put her arms around her sisters. "The answer is...

CHAPTER 8

TRAINING

I FEEL that a training montage is the best part of any movie. What is more exciting than watching people improve? The scenes are short, and the music is fast. What could be more fun?

A training montage in a book is more difficult to pull off. It's harder to capture the sense of fun, as there are few pictures and absolutely zero music.

Still, one yearns for the candy of an exciting training montage, even in a book. Therefore, while you are reading the ensuing chapter, you may want to put on a song that is very exciting to you, something uplifting and fast-paced—even though we all know that, in real life, training of any sort is always a horrible slog.

Okay. Start the song...

NOW!

THE CLASSROOM

A single sunbeam illuminated the sweltering basement laboratory. The students sat on stools at their own individual lab tables. Each had their own scalpel, microscope, and jar of dead flies. Millicent sprayed the chalkboard with a bottle labeled MY SALIVA, while the pupils stewed in their own sweat.

THE TEXTBOOKS

For Gertrude: *Unnaturalism and You*. For Eugenia: *Gemistry for Fools*. For Dee-Dee: *Fryzzics Is Fun!*

THE SUPPLIES

Millicent handed each pupil her own bottles of Millicent Quibb brand Mad Science Hair Gel™, which is formulated to "sculpt a head of individual hairs into one chaotic symphony of defiance." Active ingredient: mayonnaise.

THE UNIFORM

Tweed pants

Leather boots

Goggles

Lab coat (comes pre-stained with worm guts)

"There will be no Taffetteen in this house!" Millicent said as she locked their starched white dresses in a metal safe labeled TOXIC WASTE.

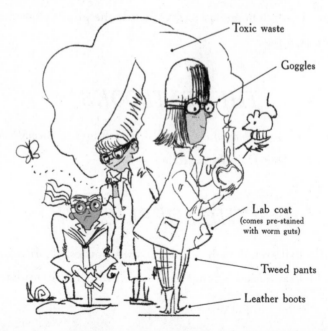

LESSON ONE

"Our first mission is to retrieve the diary of Dr. Fifi Bubblegumme, so that we can learn how to trap a Kyrgalops. These are the things you should learn before we begin," said Millicent, presenting a list that hung all the way to the floor. "But since this whole thing is time sensitive and we have to save the town from a homicidal worm TODAY, we will be focusing on a few things that I think could be useful for said mission. Now. Let us all open to page one of our textbooks."

The Porches did as they were told.

"Aaaaand, let me look at my curriculum here. Annnnnnnd, let me find my chalk. Anddddddddddddd...so. Mad science...is...Unnaturalism. There are lizards and snakes. Gemistry is...if you take a sample of malachite..."

Millicent began to sweat and shake. "Fryzzics is...I think..." She stared wide-eyed into the distance for so long that the pupils began to wonder if she had died. "I'm sorry. I can't teach right now. I feel overwhelmed. I am parched and nervous. I have to stop a Kyrgalops with the assistance of three elementary schoolchildren. The pressure is too much. I will teach soon, I promise, I just need some me-time first. Your first homework assignment is to... bring me a glass of lemonade."

Eugenia slumped over her lab table. "That's it? That's our big assignment? This school is a joke."

"Yes. You must remember, my dear, that I am operating on pure instinct, and I've been told that my instincts are bad. Anyway, Gertrude, lemons are on a tree in the greenhouse, but they might have problems." She handed Eugenia a glass that was caked in a dried bubbly black tar. "My apologies for the filthy glass, Eugenia—I haven't done dishes in a while. Dee-Dee, I'll be waiting out in the gazebo, beyond the meadow in the backyard—getting there might require a little ingenuity." And with that, Millicent ran off, leaving the children to stare and wonder where their young lives had gone wrong.

THE LEMONS

Gertrude wandered up the stairs from the basement laboratory, through the gopher-filled dining room, past the kitchen sink, which was home to a colony of seabirds, and through a glass door into the greenhouse. She thwacked through the humid thicket of jungle plants until she found an overgrown lemon tree, then picked some big yellow ripe ones. She brought the lemons back to the kitchen and sliced them in half with a knife. To her horror and private delight, the insides of the lemons were crawling with worms—red ones, with little black whiskers that looked like villain moustaches.

It would not do to serve Millicent a glass of lemonade full of red worms. Gertrude tried to pull the worms from the lemon with her fingers, but they were clinging tight with their little black moustaches, and she didn't want to squish their bodies. There had to be a way to coax them from the fruit without hurting them.

She thumbed through *Unnaturalism and You* for a solution and felt giddy looking at all the diagrams—so giddy that she started singing an impromptu song. She sang in a high and airy voice, similar to the initial whistles of a boiling tea kettle:

> *Maaaaaaaaaad science is cool*
> *And I'm doing it*
> *So maybe there's a way*
> *That I am cool*
> *But probably not*
> *But maaaaayyyyyyybeeeeeeee…*

She couldn't help but note that as she sang in this high, whistling tone, the worms used their little black moustaches to burrow deeper into the flesh of the lemon, as if to cover their ears.

"Ouch," she said. "Am I that bad at singing?"

The worms didn't answer.

"Well, what if I go low?"

And she sang in her deepest baritone:

> **WORMIES,**
> **I like you**
> **C'mere,**
> **Red wormies...**

She bellowed as low as she could, and to her great delight, the little red lemon-worms perked their heads from their citrus cave and waved their moustaches in the air, then emerged from the lemon and gathered near her to listen to the impromptu concert.

> **I am Gertruuuuuuude Pooooorch**
> **I am the coolest mad scientist everrrrrrr!!!**

Whoa! Where did *that* come from?

She stopped singing, clapped a hand over her mouth, and looked around to see if anyone had heard. Why would she say such a thing? She knew it would win her precisely zero friends in the town of Antiquarium. Then again, she couldn't shake the notion that she wanted it to be true. Then again, it was probably dumb. Then again, was it? Might it not actually...rock? Then again, it was impossible. Then again, was anything impossible, after yesterday?

THE GLASS

In the living room, Eugenia followed a ribbon of yellow tape that read CAUTION: CHEMISTY LAB. She traced the ribbon up the stairs and to a door at the end of the hallway. Inside was a pitch-dark room with tables full of gems and beakers on one side and a laundry basin on the other, with filthy clothes piled high to the ceiling.

"Ridiculous," she said. "I should be getting paid for all this." She sat at one of the tables of beakers and opened her new textbook, *Gemistry for Fools* (a title that she did NOT appreciate). She scanned the pages for an illustration that looked like the black tar on the drinking glass—tar which, upon closer observation, was composed of millions of little waving fibers.

One illustration caught her eye: a glass covered in black fuzz.

"Glass mold? Jaggedine? What is Peanutane? Where is the teacher?" she cried to no one—Millicent was off in the

Gemistry for Fools, page 872.
Glass mold.
To remove glass mold:
Titrate 10 mL of Viscous
Peanutane with
5 g Jaggedine
Pour over affected glass
Take shelter

Fig 1
To remove
glass mold

Fig 2
10 mL of Viscous
Peanutan

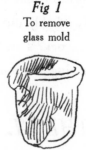

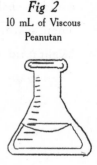

Fig 3
Titrate with
5 g Jaggedine

Fig 4
Pour over affected glass

Fig 5
TAKE SHELTER

YOU

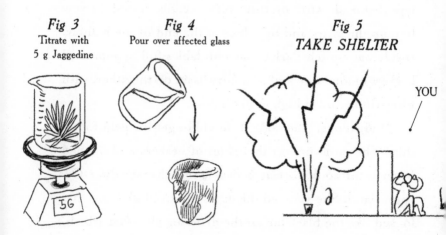

gazebo, Gertrude had gone to find lemons, and Dee-Dee could be heard wafting around the living room, talking to herself. "The teacher is supposed to say how to do it!"

Eugenia scanned rows of beakers until she spotted one labeled PEANUTANE. She walked with the dull brown liquid to a table that, to her begrudging delight, was covered in the most bizarre rocks and crystals she'd ever seen: an opalescent rock that constantly rearranged itself; a translucent rock with an actual burning fire inside; a rock that glowed blue in the dark.

"These are fake," Eugenia said to herself—though you know as well as I, perfect reader, that she secretly hoped the rocks were real.

After scanning the table, she found a chunk of jagged black crystals. A tiny brass placard next to the rock read: JAGGEDINE.

She reached to pick up the rock, but it scurried away, quick as a cockroach!

"Ah!" she cried. "Rocks do not run! Come back here!"

She hopped after the rock, checking behind beakers and under tables, until finally she spotted the hunk of Jaggedine perched atop a pile of dirty laundry.

She filled the moldy lemonade glass with 10 mL of viscous Peanutane, as per the textbook's instructions, then turned it over onto the Jaggedine. It wasn't a careful titration, but it would have to do.

For ten seconds, nothing.

Then: lightning!

The mixture crackled and sizzled and sparked and fizzled. Eugenia took cover behind a table, and when it was all over, the laundry had been reduced to a pile of charcoal, but the glass was clean as a shiny window.

Success.

Eugenia even caught herself smiling, which was something she hated to catch herself doing.

THE GAZEBO

Dee-Dee looked out over the rear deck into Millicent's backyard. The gazebo sat beyond a tall, sunny meadow full of stinging bees and sharp grasses and gnarled vines with thorns the size of railway spikes. In the distance, Millicent lay on the floor of the gazebo, nervously drumming her fingers.

"Well, well, well," Dee-Dee said, chewing her toothpick and squinting beneath the brim of her cowboy hat. "Looks like we've got a case of the old how-to's."

She kept chewing and squinting and pondering. How would she get everybody safely over the brambles? She could build three suits of armor...but that would require cutting metal, and Dee-Dee didn't feel like cutting metal. She wanted to find a more passive solution. Her destiny, after all, was to be a sea captain—not to weld.

She heard a whisper on the wind: "Build a bridge."

This had been happening more and more lately, these whispers on the wind. Dee-Dee wondered if she'd been talking to herself, or if there was a talking caterpillar living behind her ear, but she checked and there weren't any caterpillars—just spare toothpicks.

What might she use to build a bridge? She lounged on a deck chair and surveyed the environs. Now, when Dee-Dee surveyed environs, she didn't necessarily see what you or I might see: She saw shapes and patterns and possibilities. She saw colors and angles and trajectories. She saw Themath.[1] She saw spirals and she saw ratios and she saw...

A GUTTER!

Yes, there it was, plain as day: a loose copper gutter, propped against the side of the house, held there by a rope that disappeared into a chimney.

Dee-Dee moseyed back indoors and scanned for dangling ropes. There, inside a toad-infested fireplace in a corner of the conservatory, she saw a sooty rope pulled taut from above, tied to a grille.

"Bingo," she said, and untied the rope.

---

1 The universal mathematical order underlying all things.

Outside, the copper gutter whooshed through the air like a majestic falling birch and clattered onto to the steps of the gazebo. Dee-Dee had built a bridge.

She hurried outside and patted the gutter.

"Thanks for the tip!" she said.

"No problem," whispered the gutter.

The Porches teetered over the copper gutter-bridge to the gazebo, where Millicent was splayed on the floor and snoring violently.

Eugenia bent over and screamed in her ear. "WAKE UP!"

Millicent startled awake and became tangled in her laboratory skirts. There was drool dripping down her chin—a lot of it—and her cheeks were imprinted with the grain of the wood floorboards. "Yes, yes, of course, hello. I was not asleep, I was just inspecting for termites. Anyway, have you my lemonade?"

Gertrude handed the lemonade to Millicent. She turned the glass in her hand, surveying its features.

The pupils wondered if they had done enough. Typically this would be the moment when the teacher would tell them that they'd done it wrong, or that they would never succeed in life. Gertrude braced herself for impact.

"I see," Millicent said, looking rather grim. "I have some bad news for you, my pupeels."

Gertrude hung her head. It always came. The moment when the grownup decided that they were not worth educating.

"The journey to Fifi Bubblegumme's laboratory requires a group of mad scientists with innate instincts, skilled maneuvers, and daring, unconventional minds."

Gertrude held her breath. She imagined the long walk home, the familiar sting of rejection, the fetid stench of failure.

"And though I hate to say it," Millicent said, suddenly beaming bright, folding the children into her arms, "you three, my pupeels, seem to be...

READY FOR THE MISSION!!!!!!!!!!!!!"

CHAPTER 9

MME FLAMBÉ

THE LABORATORY OF Dr. Fifi Bubblegumme was hidden beneath the shop known as Mme
Flambé's Silver Spoons, a local boutique that sold one
item only:

garden hoses.

I'm kidding. They sold spoons. Hanging spoons, dangling spoons, antique spoons, new spoons, a spoon big
enough to fit a child, a spoon too small for a standard ant.
These spoons were kept on velvet pillows in sparkling glass
display cases, locked with small keys in the shape of, you
guessed it:

monkeys.

I'm kidding. The keys were shaped like silver spoons. They hung in a loop on the belt of Madame Tartine Flambé, minister of the most important rite of passage in the life of a young Antiquarian: the selection of a silver spoon.

Every child in Antiquarium, on his or her tenth birthday, got dressed in a sailor suit (the boys) or in a sailor dress (the girls) and pranced down Main Street, where everyone would clap, knowing that the blessed child was on their way to perform the sacred Spoon Selection ritual at Mme Flambé's.

Armed with this knowledge, Millicent had devised a plan of entry that was simple and implacable, whatever *implacable* means. I don't feel like looking it up right now.

1) Enter under the pretense of a tenth birthday Spoon Selection,

2) Ask Mme Flambé to open Case Number 76, the Azure Spoon of Aziza,

3) Create a distraction,

4) Open the hidden trapdoor beneath Case
Number 76, the Azure Spoon of Aziza,
and descend into the hidden laboratory of
Dr. Fifi Bubblegumme.

And so that is what they did.

The parasol-ed paraders of Antiquarium stared at the odd group walking up Main Street: three children bowing nervously, wearing improvised sailor dresses—which were some Taffetteen frocks that Millicent had pulled from a donation bin and sprayed with navy blue paint. Eugenia's dress was studded with trapped and dying mosquitos. Dee-Dee accidentally brushed past a man in a cream suit, smearing him navy. "I suppose I am in my Blue Period," she said.

"I told you we had to let these dry more!" Eugenia hissed.

"We haven't the time to watch paint dry! We must LIVE!" replied Millicent, prancing proudly like a centaur in her improvised naval commander's outfit.

Gertrude walked beside her, distracted.

"Do you remember getting your silver spoon?" Millicent said. "Are you even ten? Are you five or are you seventeen? I cannot tell the ages of children."

"Technically I'm twelve and three-quarters," Gertrude said quietly. "I never got a silver spoon 'cause I was grounded on my tenth birthday 'cause my father-uncle found a dead chipmunk under my bed that I was saving in a box to give it a proper funeral."

Millicent breathed deep and looked to the sky, as if about to bestow a piece of timeless wisdom.

With great gravitas, she said: "Come again? I couldn't hear you."

Gertrude sighed. This happened a lot. She was told that she mumbled. She took a deep breath and steadied her posture, ready to speak with import, but then thought the better of it. "Never mind."

Millicent walked on, twirling her parasol and waving at the passersby.

It wasn't until they were at the front door of Mme Flambé's that Millicent bent and whispered to Gertrude:

"I never got one either."

Millicent and her painted coterie sauntered confidently into Mme Flambé's shop, only to be greeted by a very unwelcome surprise: Imogen Crant, the glue heiress from Mrs. Wintermacher's class, was turning ten, and was midway through her spoon-picking ceremony.

She was surrounded by her parents, the Crants; her father's business associates from the Crant Glue Factory; her mother's friends from the Ladies Philanthropy Society; and some of her classmates—among them, young Lavinia-Steve, who Mrs. Crant had invited out of pity, because the other Lavinias were busy riding horses that day, and Lavinia-Steve could not be near horses, on account of the hay. Thankfully Lavinia-Steve was sneezing too much to notice her cousins in their painted sailor dresses, but still the Porches could not risk being seen, and so they turned to leave.

They were halfway out the door when Mme Flambé called to them: "Have a seat in the waiting area, *mes chéries*! I'll be with you as soon as young Miss Crant selects her spoon!"

But sitting was not an option, not with their freshly painted outfits, so the group stood with their heads bowed and prayed for a swift selection.

Gertrude's gaze wandered among the glass cases and landed in a darkened corner, on one labeled CASE NUMBER 76: THE AZURE SPOON OF AZIZA. It was a humble blue spoon encased in glass atop a marble column.

Gertrude elbowed Millicent, who squealed with delight. "Yes! Thar she blows. Now all we need is to get the key, and the entrance to Fifi Bubblegumme's laboratory will be revealed!"

"Ahem!" Mme Flambé said, and the room fell silent. "I will now preside over the Spoon Selection of Miss Imogen Crant, who is such a kind young woman,[1] and whose father, the ingenious manufacturer of Crant Glue, has been the moral backbone of this town,[2] and whose mother has raised over ten thousand dollars with the Ladies' Philanthropy Society.[3] Imogen Crant, which silver spoon will you choose?"

"Hmm...maybe...this one?" Imogen pointed to a diamond-encrusted spoon, though she couldn't quite be bothered to extend her finger.

Mme Flambé produced her infamous ring of keys, which was as large as a dinner plate and held thousands of keys, each corresponding to an individual display case. Everyone in Antiquarium knew that the joy of choosing a spoon would be tempered by the torture of watching Mme Flambé flip through those keys.

Still, Gertrude looked on the whole scene with longing. It's not that she particularly wanted a silver spoon—she could just take one from the dining room if she needed one—but she wanted what a silver spoon represented: being

---

1 Gertrude once saw Imogen Crant rip the head off a toad.

2 The Crant Glue Factory was responsible for the yearly boiling of over five hundred horses.

3 All proceeds went to the party budget for the Ladies' Philanthropy Society.

a part of the rhythm of Antiquarium, the cycle of life. Why, if you never got a silver spoon, how could you ever really call yourself an adult?

Finally, after what felt like a full calendar year, Mme Flambé handed Imogen the diamond-encrusted spoon. It glinted in the morning light, sending a miraculous spray of playful golden sunbeams across the white hats and white suits and white walls of the shop. Everyone gasped at the beauty and perfection of it.

Imogen was nonplussed. "Eh?"

Mme Flambé smiled wide while clenching her teeth. "Well then, on to the next!"

Spoon number 2: "Eh?"

Spoon number 10: "Meh?"

Spoon number 35: "Bleh."

The shadows drifted across the floor as the afternoon sun swept across the sky. Mme Flambé's hands had grown red from flipping as Imogen rejected spoon after spoon. Mr. Crant smoked a cigar, Mrs. Crant snored atop one of the counters. The Porches' legs were wobbling from hours of standing.

Eugenia gritted her teeth. "If this girl doesn't pick a spoon right now, I'm going to pick two and use them to scoop out her eyes."

Dee-Dee wept softly. "These spoons are so sad. They've all been separated from their brothers and sisters. You know, the forks and knives."

Gertrude moved to comfort her sister, when suddenly she felt the Pastramibird squirming underneath her sailor hat.

Oh dear, I've done it again. I've forgotten to mention a giant part of the scene. Please pretend I told you pages ago that this whole time, Gertrude was hiding a Pastramibird under her hat.

The Pastramibird is a thin pink bird with limp wings like flaps of boiled meat, crossed eyes, and an aversion to

Pastramibird

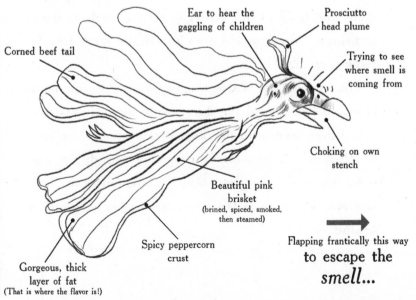

Ear to hear the gaggling of children

Prosciutto head plume

Corned beef tail

Trying to see where smell is coming from

Choking on own stench

Beautiful pink brisket
(brined, spiced, smoked, then steamed)

Spicy peppercorn crust

Gorgeous, thick layer of fat
(That is where the flavor is!)

Flapping frantically this way **to escape the** *smell...*

light. It knows peace only in caves and other dark spaces, such as beneath the sailor hats of schoolchildren, but when released into a sunny room, the Pastramibird becomes nervous and emits a thick stink like cured beef, a scent that waters the eyes and curdles the brain. If you are ever looking to clear a room in a hurry, consider the Pastramibird, though do not expect those same people to return to your house when your birthday rolls around.

The Pastramibird thrashed and writhed, and just as Mme Flambé offered Imogen her final spoon, the Pastramibird snapped—specifically, it snapped through the canvas top of Gertrude's sailor hat.

At first, no one saw the pink bird flapping flaccidly about, but they did smell the stink that descended upon them—the smell of hot brine, of boiling beef, of smoke and sinew. "Mommy, why does it smell like sandwiches?!" Imogen cried.

Imogen and her classmates dropped to the ground and army-crawled toward the door, while Mrs. Crant stampeded over them with her high-heeled boots. The businessmen hurled themselves through the front display windows, shattering the glass. Mme Flambé fell to the floor and rolled away from the store, leaving her ring of keys behind.

Outside, Lavinia-Steve watched the whole feverish ruckus with a measure of calm curiosity.

Millicent and Gertrude tried to wrangle the Pastramibird, smearing the crowd navy in the process, while Eugenia and Dee-Dee absconded with the keys to Case Number 76: The Azure Spoon of Aziza.

Eugenia shoved key after key after key into the tiny lock, to no avail. "THIS IS TORTURE!" She coughed in the meaty air, suddenly craving a loaf of rye and a bottle of mustard. Then Dee-Dee took a turn: She held the ring of keys to her ear, as though listening to the secrets of a seashell, then selected a sapphire key, which slipped easily into the lock. The front of the fluted marble pedestal that held the display folded in like an accordion, revealing a rickety platform at the top of a darkened mining shaft.

The frightened Pastramibird was clinging to a rafter overhead. Gertrude felt a funny sensation in her feet—like they were swelling, like she wanted to take her boots off and crawl up the wall to pet the bird on the head and calm it, but that was silly, as people cannot not crawl up walls!

"Pastramibird, darling, come down!" Millicent cried. "I have sunflower seeds in my pocket!"[4] The Pastramibird

---

4 Lies.

fluttered tentatively from the rafter and landed on Millicent's shoulder.

"Well!" she gulped, choking on the fetid air. "I would count that as a success! Now...

TO THE TUNNEL!"

CHAPTER 10

THE WORM TUNNEL

The Descent
By Dr. Alford Carr-Insurance

Three children and their teacher
descend beneath all hope
suspended on a platform
held by one desperate rope

too rickety for comfort.
The teacher turns the crank;
the shaft grows ever darker
and the afternoon turns to stank.

The candle flickers brighter
as the last of daylight wanes.
What streaks are these that mar the walls?
Are they claw marks?
Or bloodstains?

Dee-Dee smiles, Eugenia groans
Gertrude quakes in fear
The Pastramibird cleans its feathers
While Millicent says,
"WE'RE HERE."

I AM NERVOUS," Millicent said. "I have never been down here before. I have no way of knowing what contraptions Fifi Bubblegumme used to guard his lab. I don't want to kill someone else's children. I read a book once about a woman who dropped someone else's baby onto a brick walkway by mistake and it ruined her life and everyone else's. I hope this isn't that. Anyway. Just had to get that off my chest."

The rickety platform came to a halt. At the bottom of the old elevator shaft was a long hallway lit by sconces made out of human skulls, with little flames flicking through the nose and eye holes. A sign on the wall read:

These Skulls Were Here When I Bought This Tunnel and I Didn't Have the Money to Change Them
—Dr. F. Bubblegumme

The group tiptoed through the darkened tunnel. "Fifi Bubblegumme was a Vermologist," Millicent reminded them, "so probably any booby traps en route to the laboratory will be worm themed."

The walls and ceiling of the tunnel were lined with thousands of little holes, which none of the children wanted to really think about, least of all Eugenia, who was trying to stifle a gag.

"Eugenia, dear, are you ill?" Millicent said.

"Eugh," she gagged. "It's my trypophobia."

"Your what now?"

"I have a fear of lots of tiny holes all together, like a wasp's nest or a lotus," she replied. "Eughhhh, I can't think about it, I am gagging!"

"That sounds fake to me," said Millicent. "Is that a real fear?"

"YES!"

They pressed on. Gertrude had the bizarre feeling of being at once terrified and certain that when she looked back on the whole of her life, this day would probably rank among the greatest.

"Let us read the riddle one more time," Millicent said, and she consulted the section of Fifi Bubblegumme's diary labeled KEYPAD INSTRUCTIONS FOR MY LAB.

"Open the lock with the azure spoon
The laboratory will be your boon
But be quick, for after a minute
There may be some visitors in it."

Gertrude shuddered to think of who the visitors might be, but Millicent had been assuring them all afternoon that they would spend no more than sixty seconds inside the laboratory.

"What happens after sixty seconds?" Eugenia had asked, trying to appear casual.

"I do not know," Millicent had said. "But let us do our best to not find out."

Finally, the group reached the end of the tunnel, where they came upon a door, which had been carved from a solid slab of beautiful, swirling blue rock.

"Veinite," Eugenia said. "Interesting."

Millicent smiled slyly, having caught Eugenia in a rare

moment of sincere interest. "Where did you read about Veinite?"

Eugenia bristled, not about to be pegged for anything other than an aloof and annoyed person. "Not that I care, but it was in the textbook you gave. The crystals rearrange themselves in the presence of azure. Again, not that I care."

"Would you like to do the honors, then?" Millicent asked, handing Eugenia the Azure Spoon of Aziza.

Eugenia rolled her eyes and, having forgotten all about her trypophobia and the tiny holes, placed the spoon into an opening in the door. At once, the crystals of Veinite began to curl like ringlets of hair, and the door crumpled in on itself.

Millicent and the Porches had to admit that it was one of the more beautiful things that had ever graced their eyeballs. They stood there for ten seconds or so, observing the slow caving of crystal, marveling at how something so solid could be so summarily rearranged, almost like life itself.

"Wait!" Eugenia cried, yanking the group from their reverie. "We only have sixty seconds, remember! Run!" She checked her pocket watch. "FIFTY SECONDS REMAINING!"

The group burst into Fifi Bubblegumme's laboratory, a stone chamber strewn with old glass terrariums, hundreds of empty silkworm cocoons, and reams and reams of silk—spun, ostensibly, by a now-defunct colony of silkworms. In one corner there was a pile of books as high as the ceiling, thousands of leather-bound books, all labeled DIARY.

"Which one is the right diary?" Gertrude cried.

"THIRTY-SEVEN SECONDS REMAINING!"

"I DON'T KNOW!" Millicent shouted. "Just take them all! Pile them into your pockets!"

They stuffed as many leather-bound diaries as they could into their Taffetteen pockets, which was not many. Meanwhile, the walls began to quake, and dust shook from the ceiling.

"FOURTEEN SECONDS REMAINING!"

Millicent looked around for a solution, then, in a panic, cried: "Dee-Dee, darling, make a machine!"

Dee-Dee surveyed the room from beneath the brim of her cowboy hat. Cocoons, terrariums, reams of silk—not much for making a diary-carrying machine, but if anyone could do it, it was Dee-Dee.

"Got it."

She wobbled under the weight of a bolt of blue silk as she pulled it from the pile. It was stitched together at the ends, forming a big band. She knew that she could use the silk to construct a conveyor belt and lay the diaries on it—but how would the belt be conveyed?

"ONE SECOND REMAINING!"

Then, zero. Silence.

"What happens now?" Gertrude whispered.

"Now we wait," Millicent said gravely.

All was still.

Then, little pitters and patters.

"Where are the visitors?" Gertrude whispered in terror.

Eugenia, looking up at the horrible holes in the ceiling and in the walls, began to gag. "I am going to barf," she said. "I am barfing. Oh my gourd, I am barfing."

From the holes emerged hundreds and hundreds of tiny silkworms, gray and furry. They fell like grains of rice at a wedding and writhed on the ground. They fell like a spring rain, pelting the floor, landing in the pupils' hair. White wormy worms, wriggling everywhere. Every surface was alive and churning.

Millicent's chest heaved as she tried to control her

breathing. "This is fine," she said brightly. "This is all in the course of a normal school! The school is going well!"

The group stood two feet deep in a pool of worms, while more slopped from the ceiling. Gertrude could feel them burrowing through her hair, up her sleeves, and down her socks. She wanted to wade through the horde to get to safety but didn't want to crush any of the poor things underfoot, so she stayed where she was, figuring maybe it was her destiny to be buried alive in a grave of worms.

She considered screaming, but she didn't want to appear terrified in front of her little sisters, so she turned her scream into a single high-pitched, operatic note.

A few of the worms that were worming around in her hair suddenly leaped to the ground, as if trying to escape the sound.

"Jeez, my voice isn't *that* bad!" Then she remembered the lemonade-worms and how they were repelled by the sound of high-pitched singing. Might these silkworms be the same?

Gertrude took a breath from deep in her core and sang as high and loud as she could: *"Azure Spoon of Aziz-zaaaaaaaaaaa...!"*

The worms slithered away from her as fast as their segmented tube bodies could carry them.

"Everyone, sing!" Gertrude shouted. "Sing high!"

Millicent, never one to turn down an opportunity to perform, cleared her throat and sang an Italian aria about unrequited love. The worms fled en masse.

Eugenia, who had never deigned to part her lips in song, offered a reedy rendition of "You're a Grand Old Flag."

Dee-Dee was not one for singing. She was too busy studying Themath[1] of the scene—the angles, the forces, the torques, the propulsions, the forward churning of the worms...Huzzah! What better way to power a silk conveyor belt?

Dee-Dee fed the blue silk over the swarm, and the worms churned it forward. She tipped her cowboy hat to the wriggling pistons of her impromptu motor. "All in a day's work, boys."

The Porches all pitched in to pile the leather diaries onto the conveyor belt, except for Eugenia, who was too ill from the sight of worms and tiny holes, so they piled Eugenia onto the conveyor belt as well.

Loading the diaries into the trunk of the Gerbilcar was a tedious misadventure all its own, as is always the case when

---

1 Reminder: The universal order underlying all things.

one has to load things into the trunk of a car. Suffice it to say that Millicent and her pupils sped away with their hard-won cargo just as Mme Flambé returned with the police, where she found nothing out of place, save for a few stray worms wriggling on the floor.

Meanwhile, across the street, Ursula Wintermacher enjoyed a cup of tea and watched the diary-filled scene unfold through a pair of opera glasses.

"Fascinating," she said. "Now I see where those three little rejects ran off to that day. Looks like Millicent Quibb has gotten herself some pupils!"

At the same time, Lavinia-Steve was peering around the corner, wondering why the three children loading books into a strange car looked a lot like...

HER COUSINS!

_____

CHAPTER 11

THE DIARY OF FIFI BUBBLEGUMME

MILLICENT AND HER PUPILS sat amongst piles of ancient leather diaries in various states of decay. They had already combed through one thousand seven hundred and fifty-six of them. It was 8:00 PM, and no information about the Kyrgalops had presented itself.

"Is it possible," Eugenia said through gritted teeth, "that this Dr. Fifi Bubblegumme somehow knew everything about every single unnatural worm *other* than the Kyrgalops?"

Millicent thought a moment. "Yes, I suppose."

Eugenia slumped over onto the floor. Dee-Dee had used rubber bands and a coat hanger to construct a machine that would hold her eyelids open, but she was snoring, so one couldn't tell if she was actually reading or not.

That's when Gertrude, half-asleep herself, opened an unassuming, unlabeled brown diary with fragile pages. She scanned the tiny script until finally she saw what the group had been looking for all those hours. Was it a mirage? No! There it was, plain as day!

On the subject of the Kyrgalops

"I...I think...I found it!" Gertrude called out groggily.

She began to read aloud, straining to decipher the flowery cursive of Dr. Fifi Bubblegumme.

"I was born a poor boy in Transylvania in 1624. My mother was dead, and my father was a grape-stomper. For dinner, we typically shared a single bean."

Eugenia yawned. "Skip to the Kyrgalops, please. I don't need his whole life story."

Gertrude peered farther down the page.

"One day, while foraging in a mossy grotto, I discovered a den of the most wonderful worms: a worm that could fly, a worm that could become flat as paper, a worm that could balloon into a ball and roll down a hill! These worms became my playmates, my confidantes—"

"Again," Eugenia said with a yawn, "I don't need to know what this man had for breakfast, just get to the Kyrg."

Gertrude scanned even farther down.

"When my father discovered my colony of fabulous worms, he

brought me and my worm friends to the palace of the evil King Radu.

"'I will give you two dollars for the boy and the worms.' My father was so poor and thought I might have a better life at the castle, so he took the deal—"

"Get to the Kyrgalops, already!" Eugenia said.

"Ah!" Gertrude said. "Here it is."

"One day, King Radu came to me in a blind fury.

"'Doctor Fifi,' he said. 'Please make me a worm that can eat through stone. Good King Nicolai of Wallachia has made a wall around his city five boulders thick. I need to get through there so I can kill everybody.'

"'King, can I ask you something?' I ventured. 'You've already killed so many people in so many cities. Have you thought about why you feel the need to keep doing that?'

"'You impudent wretch!' said King Radu. 'My father was mean to me, of course! Now make me a worm that can eat through stone, or else...I will... kill your father!'

"So, you see, I had no choice. I crossbred many different unnatural worms, until at last the day came when I hatched a fearsome worm, long as an anaconda and thick as a cow, sheathed in hard scarlet scales, with a round mouth lined with teeth harder than diamond. I called it the 'Kyrgalops.'

"No reason. I just thought it was a good name.

"As King Radu unleashed the Kyrgalops on city after innocent city, I fled with my remaining Kyrgalops eggs to the town of Antiquarium, so that I could make sure they never terrorized the earth again."

"I am sad now, and that annoys me," said Eugenia. "Just tell us about the worm."

Gertrude read on. *"The Kyrgalops's preferred habitat is salt water, where it can live harmoniously on a diet of algae and old shells. The male of the species lives as a parasite in the stomach of the female, never growing larger than a hamster...,"* Gertrude read, "and then the rest of this sentence is smeared in mustard, or at least I hope it's mustard."

"Fine, skip that part," said Millicent. "We've no time for the gender politics of worms."

"The Kyrgalops becomes docile in the presence of the legendary Panacea Slug. What is a Panacea Slug?" Gertrude asked.

Millicent turned to Gertrude and spoke in low, jubilant tones. "Oh, a wonderful creature," she said. "A legendary creature. Part human, part slug. Its slime is a curative for disease. An amazing creature."

"Wow," Gertrude whispered. "I actually love slugs."

"As well you should," said Millicent. And Gertrude felt full of something, the warm feeling you get when you say something weird and someone else says, "I know, me too!"

She read on. *"The Kyrgalops can survive on a diet of crushed rock. However, it cannot resist the smell and taste of one softer item in particular: the small canine known in some communities as...*

the Bichon Frise.

The worm can be lured to any location by a congregation of said dogs."

"Aha!" said Millicent. "That's why it bit the ponytail off the marble statue of the bichon! It wasn't hungry for marble at all—it was hungry for the dog!"

The four paused to consider the gruesome implications.

"Well, that's great," Eugenia said, breaking the silence, "but how do we trap it?"

Gertrude read on.

"The worm can crunch through any type of metal or stone, except for the rare unnatural mineral Prismuth, which can only be found pearled inside certain oysters off the coast of Taiwan."

"Dingdong!" Millicent cried. "Prismuth! Of course! We simply have to build a cage out of Prismuth, then sneak into Mrs. Wintermacher's office, transfer the Kyrgalops into the cage, carry it out to sea, *et voilà!* The town is saved!"

"Hold your horses, woman," said Eugenia. "Where are we going to find this exceptionally rare mineral?"

Millicent thought a moment. "I do not know yet. This will require a night's sleep. But for now, we must replenish our strength, with the greatest of life's offerings."

An hour later, the Porches were still waiting anxiously at the dining room table while Millicent clattered around the kitchen. It sounded like she was playing basketball with a set of pots and pans. A familiar smell wafted in from the stovetop—the smell of tomato sauce.

Finally, Millicent returned with a round tray, on top of which sat a hot circle of bread slathered with sauce and cheese and dotted with olives. "Here it is: the greatest of life's offerings."

She set the tray on the table and breathed in the smell. "There is only one thing in this world, my pupeels, that can truly lift the spirit, fill the belly, and soothe the mind—and that thing is...say it with me..."

The Porches were silent.

"PIZZA," said Millicent. "That thing is pizza."

The Porches had never had a slice of pizza, as it was 1911 and pizza had not yet taken a firm foothold in the continental United States.

Gertrude took the first bite. It was, in fact, the finest thing she had ever tasted: it was the taste of warmth, of comfort, of bliss. Eugenia finished her slice in three bites. Dee-Dee pressed two slices together, then folded those in half, then in half again, to form a pizza layer cake.

Gertrude ate happily, exploring the many magical properties of mozzarella cheese, then remembered that there were still pressing matters at hand.

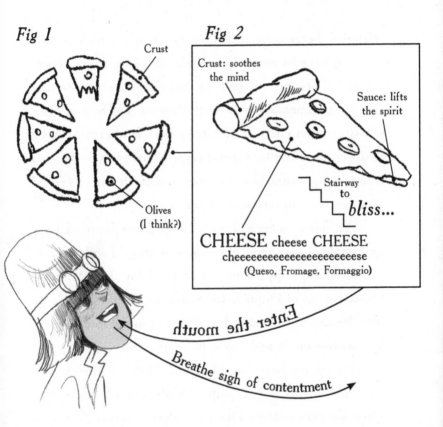

Fig 1

Crust

Olives
(I think?)

Fig 2

Crust: soothes
the mind

Sauce: lifts
the spirit

Stairway
to
bliss...

CHEESE cheese CHEESE
cheeeeeeeeeeeeeeeeeeeeeese
(Queso, Fromage, Formaggio)

Enter the mouth

Breathe sigh of contentment

"Ms. Quibb, I've been meaning to ask—who is Talon Sharktūth?" Gertrude asked.

"Ugh!" Millicent spit her pizza onto her plate. "Vile. I hate to ruin a perfectly good pizza party, but if you must know—and indeed you must—Talon Sharktūth was the founder of the KRA. He was a psychopath, a narcissist, a dental train wreck. They say his teeth were upside-down triangles, because he had done experiments with sharks! They say his eyes were black—again, from the shark experiments! They say he had no tongue—unrelated to the shark experiments! There were rumors that he had been working on an elixir of life. They say that after the fire he fled underground to a secret vault in order to perfect his immortality serum, only to emerge when the time is right! May that vault never see the light of day."

The four sat soberly, until Millicent threw her pizza down on her plate. "But let us not wallow in worry! I wish to commend you, my pupils. This is the second day of the Millicent Quibb School of Etiquette for Young Ladies of Mad Science and already you have absorbed plenty of useful information. You are fine pupils and...well, it's sappy. Never mind."

"Please stop here," said Eugenia. "I do not do sap."

"Neither do I, but, well...I stole you all something, when we were at Mme Flambé's Silver Spoons." Millicent rolled her eyes to make it seem like it wasn't a big deal. She pulled three silver spoons from the pocket of her lab coat and tossed them unceremoniously on the table. "There. You said none of you ever got a silver spoon on your tenth birthdays like all the other children in Antiquarium. So I stole spoons for you. That's all."

Dee-Dee cradled the spoon to her cheek. Eugenia put

it in her pocket and nodded, trying with all her might not to smile or feel anything about it.

Gertrude looked at her reflection on the back of the spoon. Her hair was wild and filled with worms, her lab coat was wrinkled and filthy, and yet she looked...like herself. She felt a lump in her throat, a certain warmth, as if there was a parenthesis around the four of them, punctuation that said GROUP. And she was a part of it. It felt so wonderful, to be a real part of something.

"See? Mad scientists can have silver spoons too. But we do it on our own terms. Okay, enough mush. Eat your pizza."

Before Gertrude could begin to express her gratitude, a fresh horror emerged. As Dee-Dee opened her mouth to burp, a vine started growing out of it, wending its way through the air like smoke from an after-dinner cigar.

While Gertrude and Eugenia screamed, Dee-Dee watched with a detached sort of wonder.

"Oh dear," Millicent said calmly. "I seem to have used Rapier Vine seeds instead of olives. They look so similar—I have got to get a label maker! No matter—let us turn this mistake into a learning opportunity! What you see here are Rapier Vines in action. They can be very useful. They can even snap iron bars in two!"

The vines curled over the arms of the iron chandelier overhead, cracking it in half.

Eugenia and Gertrude started gagging, trying to get rid of the pizza they'd just eaten.

"Help Dee-Dee!" Gertrude cried.

"Help ME!" Eugenia cried.

Millicent just scowled and poured everyone a glass of orange juice. "Oh, don't be so uptight, just drink this. The vine can't survive in acid."

The Porches guzzled the orange juice, and the vines were no more, and all was well again, except for Millicent, who seemed upset.

"For shame." She hung her head. "Orange juice and pizza. It's...so wrong. It isn't done."

The children burst into laughter, the kind of laughter you can only laugh after you've been screaming.

"Here, girls—you should each have your own packet of Rapier Vine seeds. Keep them in your pockets, for a rainy day."

And thus was the rhythm of life at the Millicent Quibb School of Etiquette for Young Ladies of Mad Science. Danger, laughter, danger, laughter. Was their teacher a benevolent guide, or would she accidentally kill them all? Where would they find enough Prismuth to make a cage big enough to trap the Kyrgalops? Would they ever meet a Panacea Slug? These and other questions plagued the pupils.

But now was not the time for pensive wallowing. It had been a good day, and the only thing to do was be glad of it.

And that, my dear reader, is exactly what Mrs. Wintermacher thought to herself as she eavesdropped outside Millicent Quibb's kitchen window.

She surveyed her spy notes. "*Kyrgalops cannot resist the smell and taste of the bichon frise.*"

"Yes, that's it!" she whispered to herself. "That's exactly it! That is how we will lure the worm to the desired location!

WE WILL USE THE BICHONS."

CHAPTER 12

THE TEA PARTY

IT WAS 10:00 PM when the three exhausted Porches filed through the front door of the Parquette house. Aunt Desdemona and Grantie Lettuce were doing needlepoint, and Uncle Ansel had laid out his entire collection of cuff links on the floor in order to catalog them.

"How was school today, dears?" said Aunt Desdemona.

"You certainly were there long enough!" said Uncle Ansel, crawling through a lake of cuff links.

"Oh, yeah, she basically kept us extra to learn about, um, ironing napkins," said Gertrude. The girls were still picking pizza from their teeth, but they were wearing their Taffetteen dresses (which were plenty crisp after being stored in Millicent's toxic waste cabinet), and their hair was brushed straight (after a thorough deworming with Millicent's deworming comb).

Aunt Desdemona was impressed by the discipline and rigor and seriousness that seemed to have befallen her adoptive nieces, who had never before brushed their hair. Even their posture was different. They stood taller, their voices were clearer, they seemed more poised. "Gertrude, you are looking...well!" Aunt Desdemona said.

Grantie Lettuce leaned in and whispered to Aunt Desdemona. "Don't be a...Silly Sally," she whispered.

"But I think the children seem much improved!" Aunt Desdemona whispered back.

Grantie Lettuce went back to her needlepoint, trailing her eyes on the Porches. "Sally."

Aunt Desdemona turned back to the children. "Well then! I think soon I'd like to meet this Marjory Questions who is whipping you three into shape. In fact, I think you should call her up right now and ask her to come to tea...

TOMORROW!"

No.

It couldn't be so.

Millicent, in their house, with her fake voices and neon dresses, chitchatting with their aunt?

It was a recipe for disaster.[1]

This was a terrifying proposition, and yet, given the wildness of Aunt Desdemona's eyes, they knew there was no choice, and so they hurried to the upstairs study and rang Millicent Quibb.

"Shello?" she croaked.

Gertrude whispered nervously into the receiver. "Yes, um, Miss Quibb, er, Professor Quibb, this is Gertrude Porch, one of the girls from your new school—?"

"Yes, I know who you are, I was just with you, go on."

"So, our aunt Desdemona thinks we're going to kind of a more 'normal' or 'typical' etiquette school run by a lady named 'Marjory Questions,' which is a cool name you came up with, and, funny story—well, sort of more quirky, I guess—?"

"Marjory Questions has to come to tea," Eugenia said flatly, taking the phone from Gertrude. "Tomorrow, two PM."

"Ahhhh, perfect!" said Millicent. "I'll be there with literal bells on!"

---

1 And a delicious one at that. See *Pimm's Recipes for Disaster*, page 45, "Mad Scientist Has Tea with Fancy Aunt."

"Yes but, um, the, the *rub*, as it were," said Gertrude, "is that you're more of a...Millicent Quibb type, if that makes sense?"

"Say no more!" Millicent said. "It will be my greatest performance to date! Oh joy, a GIG! I must go, I have to select my wig and costume for the role. See you soon! Or rather, *Marjory Questions* will see you soon!"

Eugenia slowly replaced the phone receiver. "Well, we've had a good run. See you guys in Austria."

They looked up to see Lavinia-Steve staring at them through a crack in the door.

This was something of a metaphysical impossibility, as all Lavinias go to sleep at 6:30 PM sharp, with mud masks on their faces and cucumbers on their eyes—and yet, there she was. How long had she been standing there? What had she heard?

"Hey, you guys!" she said, smiling nervously. Her voice was bubbly and sweet, like fizzy lemonade. "I just heard you up here and I was like, 'Hmm, I wonder what they're up to,' so I thought I'd come say hi. 'Cause, like, I saw you at Mme Flambé's today—achoo!—and you were with your new teacher and she looks cool, and it seems like your new school is actually much funner than Mrs. Wintermacher's and—aaaaaaaaachoo!—I guess, I just wanted to know if you ever wanted to, I guess, hang out? Like, the four of us?"

Gertrude softened. None of the Lavinias had ever expressed even a droplet of interest in spending time with the Porches. Gertrude searched her sweet face for a trace of bitterness but could find none. In fact, all Gertrude wanted to do was give her a hug. Was it possible, according to the laws of the known universe? Could a Porch and a Lavinia, under the right conditions, actually…join in friendship?

According to Eugenia, the answer was a resounding NO.

"You're in way over your head, girlie!" she barked. "Don't go sniffing around stuff you can't handle!"

Lavinia-Steve's smile gave way to a whimper. A tear appeared in her eye. A Lavinia, crying tears of rejection at the hands of a Porch? Even with all the Hornflowers and the Pastramibirds and the Kyrgalopses, it was somehow the strangest thing Gertrude had seen all week—and the saddest.

Their fancy little cousin ran off sneeze-crying.

"Geez, Eug—you could have been a *little* nicer," said Gertrude, upset that her fragile new friendship had shattered before she'd even taken it out of the box.

Eugenia smoothed her dress and cracked her knuckles. "We have no time for Lavinias! We have to focus! We must prepare ourselves so that we may survive…

THE MOST AWKWARD TEA PARTY IN HISTORY!"

It was a glorious, sunny afternoon in the garden, complete with the buzzing of bees and the flapping of butterflies—but to the Porches, even the drifting of dandelion seeds looked like trouble.

They sat at the tea table in excruciating silence while Aunt Desdemona tapped her fingers on the rim of her tea-cup. There were deviled quail eggs, cucumber sandwiches cut down to the size of thimbles, and monogrammed shortbread cookies, but no one was eating—they were too busy waiting for Marjory Questions.

"She's late!" Aunt Desdemona said. It was 2:01 PM. "What kind of an etiquette teacher is late for a tea party—?"

Suddenly Millicent burst in, wearing a radiant dress of pink Taffetteen and a hat of pink tulle. Taken as a whole, the ensemble gave the effect of cotton candy.

"Good afternoon, Madame Parquette, and please do forgive my lateness!" Millicent said. "Oh, the marvelous things I have heard about you! You are the stuff of legend. Kindness and wit in equal measure. The staunchest of women. Grace on a plate. Good afternoon. I am Marjory Questions."

Aunt Desdemona blushed as Millicent bent to kiss her hand.

"Children, please stand while women are introducing themselves to one another!" Millicent barked. Her pupils marveled at the magnificent performance.

Millicent settled at the table next to Aunt Desdemona. "NOW you may sit," she said. "And do not speak for the rest of the afternoon. Adult women are talking."

The Porches nodded and sipped their tea.

"Thank you so much for the invitation, my dear Desdemona," said Millicent. "I have been working with the children and have found them wholly unpleasant, though they have improved moderately with the use of mild insults, sturdy aloofness, and constant unspoken disapproval. Wouldn't you say so, children?"

The Porches nodded earnestly.

"I knew it," said Aunt Desdemona, glowing. "I knew you would be the woman for the job. I have been trying to bend these little unfortunates into compliance for years, and here you've managed in a few days!"

"It is my gift," said Millicent. "Speaking of gifts: Children, would you march over to my car and fetch my purse? I've forgotten my tea gift for Aunt Desdemona."

The Porches did as they were told.

"She's amazing!" Gertrude whispered.

"She's up to something," said Eugenia.

Inside Millicent's purse was an ancient book entitled *Unnatural Gems for Costume Jewelry*, with a red feather jutting out the middle. The pupils opened the book and saw a paragraph circled many times around in aggressive pen marks.

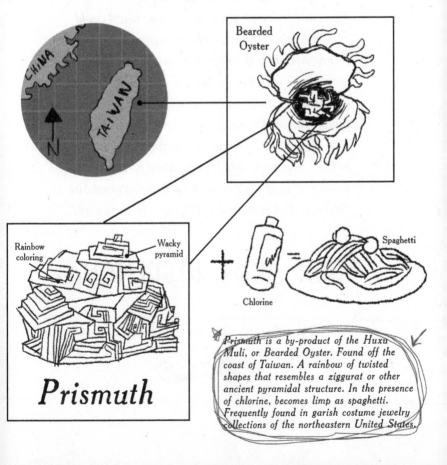

Bearded Oyster

Rainbow coloring

Wacky pyramid

Prismuth

Chlorine

Spaghetti

Prismuth is a by-product of the Huxu Muli, or Bearded Oyster. Found off the coast of Taiwan. A rainbow of twisted shapes that resembles a ziggurat or other ancient pyramidal structure. In the presence of chlorine, becomes limp as spaghetti. Frequently found in garish costume jewelry collections of the northeastern United States.

"Well, that's fine," Eugenia whined, "but where are we supposed to find it?"

"Read the fine print," Dee-Dee said, pulling out a magnifying glass.

And indeed, Millicent had written a minuscule note in the margins:

> *My Pupeels: You know, many years ago I dined alone at a fish restaurant in town so that I could spy on a group of ladies who I suspected might be involved with the KRA. It turned out they were not—it was just a book club. Also, my halibut was dry. It was a useless evening all around. BUT—in reading about Prismuth last night, I remembered that I had seen the mineral in person only once before: on a truly ugly brooch, worn by one of the women at that table on that very useless night at that very fish restaurant. Who was that woman?*

YOUR AUNT DESDEMONA.

"See?" Eugenia said. "I knew she was up to something."

When the Porches returned with the purse, Millicent and Aunt Desdemona could be heard giggling inside the house. "Great," Eugenia said dryly. "They're bonding."

They followed the giggles up the grand staircase and down the hall, where the ladies were admiring Aunt Desdemona's walk-in closet. It was lined with hundreds of drawers filled with necklaces, hatpins, pocket watches, silk scarves, and the like.

"Ansel bought me those gloves when we were in Morocco visiting the prince," Aunt Desdemona gushed.

"You know the prince?" Millicent laughed. "Oh, how small this little teeny world is! I can't believe it! I wintered with the prince as a girl! At his chalet in Freihoffensdorfer und Escargot! What an awful skier he is!"

"My dear Miss Questions, you are an enigma and a delight!"

Millicent clutched her heart. "I could actually cry. It has been my life's only wish to be an enigma and a delight."

Millicent gasped as she plucked a piece of jewelry from the drawer—an emerald brooch in the shape of a frog. "This is stunning! Where did one find such a priceless treasure?"

Aunt Desdemona curtsied. "Ansel bought this for me when he boated down the Ganges."

"What a well-traveled man!" Millicent said. "What brings him to these marvelous locales?"

"Oh, ivory, of course," Aunt Desdemona said proudly. "He murders elephants for ivory. He also murders other animals...tigers, rhinoceroses, the like. He is truly brave."

Millicent breathed deep through gritted teeth. Gertrude could tell that she wanted to scream, but Marjory Questions would do no such thing, so instead she squealed with delight.

"Ahh! AMAZING! What a man!" It was then that Millicent pointed to a small brooch at the back of the case. "Now, tell me about this beauty."

"Oh, this old thing?" said Aunt Desdemona. "Ugh. It looks like some kind of garish rainbow pyramid. Ansel got it for me while he was killing dolphins off the coast of Taiwan. They told him it was a rare pearl, but I think it looks like junk."

"Hmm. A rainbow pyramid!" Millicent said loudly, staring at her pupils. "A rare pearl, found off the coast of Taiwan...here in your collection of jewelry? How interesting."

The Porches gasped. Prismuth!

"I hate it," said Aunt Desdemona. "And look! He brought back a whole load of the stuff." Aunt Desdemona opened a narrow door, and a whole closet full of rainbow brooches made of Prismuth tumbled onto the floor. "See?"

The Porches could barely contain their glee, and neither could Millicent. "Well, this is certainly the finest collection of brooches I have ever seen. Now, would you mind showing me your ottomans? Pupils, why don't you restock these shelves while the fine ladies do their fine lady things?"

Aunt Desdemona pushed past the Porches, and Millicent followed, nose in the air.

Then, when Aunt Desdemona was down the hallway, Millicent darted back and whispered to her pupils:

"STEAL THE BROOCHES."

The Porches smiled deviously.

Aunt Desdemona didn't hear her, of course—but someone else did. Someone who was home from school with severe allergies; someone still nursing the wounds of rejection at the hands of Eugenia; someone holed up in the next room, trying not to sneeze. Someone named...

LAVINIA-STEVE.

ENTR·ACTE 2

YOU ARE HEROES for reading this far, really. Sooooo many characters, soooooo many weird scenarios. The visualizer in your mind is working so hard that it's probably overheated and smoking at this point. You have done well, my valiant reader. Let us enjoy a small break in all that visualizing, and allow me to demonstrate to you how it was that Eugenia and Dee-Dee used the Prismuth brooches that they stole from Aunt Desdemona's closet to construct a cage for the Kyrgalops, a cage through which it could not bite.

And yes—the use of illustrations also gets me out of having to painstakingly describe this part, but I assure you that's not why I'm doing it. My work ethic is as gorgeous as the wood paneling in my study, and I, G. Edwina Candlestank, would NEVER, EVER, L'EVER shirk my duties as your guide through these tales, which are necessary for your very survival!

I'm going to hand the paper over to the illustrator now and go watch TV.

HOW TO BUILD A PRISMUTH CAGE

1. Eugenia carefully dissolved the Prismuth chunks in a vat of carbonic acid.

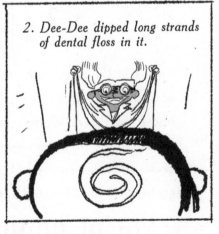

2. Dee-Dee dipped long strands of dental floss in it.

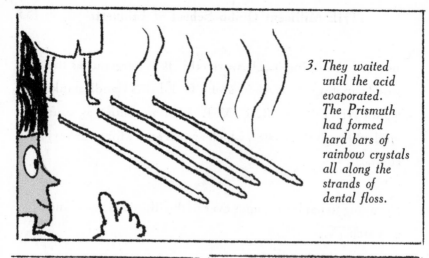

3. They waited until the acid evaporated. The Prismuth had formed hard bars of rainbow crystals all along the strands of dental floss.

4. They welded the bars into a long rectangular cage, like a crab trap but the size of a small bus.

5. Eugenia and Dee-Dee did a dance that they choreographed for the occasion.

I'm back. I'm refreshed. Now, if you'll remember, Millicent and the Porches are planning to return to the belly of the beast, Mrs. Wintermacher's school, in order to trap the Kyrgalops in their Prismuth cage and carry it out to the ocean. Will they succeed? I pray your visualizer is ready to get back to work, because by gourd...

YOU'RE GOING TO NEED IT.

CHAPTER 13

THE SECRET MEETING

DRINK THIS," said Millicent.

She handed cups of steaming brown stuff to the Porch sisters, who were sitting on the guinea pig massage chairs in her living room, loosening their muscles to prepare for the heist.

They had everything they needed. They would sneak into Mrs. Wintermacher's office, pry open the bars, lure the unsuspecting worm into the Prismuth cage with a fluffy white throw pillow, and release the worm into to the bay, where it would live out its days in peace.

The Porches were reticent to drink the brown liquid. "Um, Ms. Quibb, it's not that we don't all love your snacks and drinks, per se," Gertrude said delicately, "but I think, well, we might all be a little burned from the Rapier Vine/ pizza incident."

Millicent hung her head and sighed deeply. "And yet you must drink. We are about to embark on a long, dangerous mission for which none of us is qualified. The drink I have set before you is the secret juice of a rare and unnatural bean, which will give you strength, agility, and heightened awareness. You will be transformed into acrobats, safe-crackers, ninjas. You will be, in a word, adults."

The Porches stared with wonder and terror at the steaming brown liquid.

"What is it called?" Eugenia whispered, in a rare moment of reverence.

Millicent pulled on her coat. "I call it...

COFFEE.

Now. Let's go get that big red worm before it gets the town."

The four rode down Main Street in Millicent's Gerbilcar, with the humungous rectangular Prismuth cage tied to the roof.

"Can't you go any faster?" Eugenia grumbled. The smelly, screeching car inched along the street while a mile of regular cars beeped angrily behind it.

"I cannot," Millicent declared. "The Prismuth cage is so light that it will blow away in the breeze if we're not careful."

The morning shoppers and strollers of Antiquarium looked on in confusion at the slow car with the bus-sized rainbow cage tied on top.

Gertrude was terrified that Aunt Desdemona and Uncle Ansel might see them, as they were supposed to be attending a special Saturday lecture series at the Marjory Questions School—but Millicent was undaunted.

"It's for a party!" she shouted gaily to the crowd. "We're having a big party, and this shimmering rainbow cage is to house the dancing revelers as we move through the street!" She was improvising, of course, but she had in fact birthed an idea that would later become the party bus. But that is beyond the scope of this book.

The passersby reacted with distaste and confusion. "What are they doing with that rainbow monstrosity?" "Who ever saw such a thing?"

"Clap," Millicent urged under her breath. "Clap and whoop. They'll think it's a parade."

"I will not clap and whoop!" Eugenia said.

But Gertrude had come to trust Millicent's bizarre

instincts, at least some of the time, and began to clap. She stood in the front seat and shouted meekly to the people of Antiquarium. "Yay!!! A parade!"

The passersby saw the cheering children and the glinting sun on the rainbow cage and couldn't help but begin to yelp with joy themselves. "Yayyy!" they cheered back. "A parade!"

Gertrude smiled, having never been the cause of a celebration before, albeit a baseless one.

"See?" Millicent said. "One can make a parade out of very little."

Millicent and the Porches gathered in the bushes beneath the window of Mrs. Wintermacher's office.

The window was closed, it being a Saturday, and so they had to find an alternative means of entry. "We now find ourselves," said Millicent, "in an old-fashioned quandary. How do we get in? That is the million-dollar question. Do we mix up a quart of brick melter? Of course to do that we'd first need to grind up a pound of Vampire Peppers, and that always results in severe burns and loss of vision. Or then again we could always bore through the skylight using a pair of Roof Voles, but I only have baby Roof Voles right now, and we'd need to feed them a whole horse in order for them to mature, and I only have a half horse in the freezer...or then again we could always build a giant drill—"

"The front door is open," Eugenia said flatly, glancing over at the gaping front entrance.

"Good, good," said Millicent. "Always useful to weigh one's options, but yes, let us use the front door."

A small army of maids and janitors filed through the front entrance carting various mops and brooms and soaps. Millicent and her pupils filed in after them, then peeled off and tiptoed toward Mrs. Wintermacher's empty office.

Millicent locked the office door behind them. Dee-Dee readied the white pillow that would serve as a decoy bichon, while Eugenia and Gertrude carefully removed the portrait of Mrs. Wintermacher, revealing the hole in the wall behind it.

To their great dismay, they found that the bars were gone...

AND SO WAS THE KYRGALOPS!

"Where, um, where did it go?" Gertrude whispered, shivering as she squinted into the empty void.

Millicent calmly sunk to the floor, curling into a ball underneath her skirts.

"Well, I'm out," she mumbled from underneath a pile of wool.

"What do you mean, 'you're out'?" Eugenia growled. "You can't be out—you're the adult!"

"Let me tell you something about adults," Millicent murmured, now fully cocooned in pantaloons. "Adults don't know that much. It's comforting to think that they do, and they certainly act like they do, but no one really knows what to do, when it comes down to it, so I'm giving in to the fact that I'm fully lost. I want you girls to continue on, but I am, as I said before, out—"

"Shhh!" Gertrude said, leaning into the empty void. "Sorry, I didn't mean to cut you off, I was enjoying your speech, but I hear something in here. I think it's...voices?"

She craned her ear farther into the empty tunnel, where she could in fact just barely hear the dim din of voices.

Her mind told her to run, but her feet, which seemed to have a mind of their own lately, felt like they were melting toward the tunnel—and so she stood on Mrs. Wintermacher's chair and hoisted her entire self up into the tunnel.

"What are you doing?!" Eugenia cried, tugging at Gertrude's skirt. "You'll get killed and then I'll be sisterless, except for Dee-Dee, who is great, but I need both!"

"A three-legged stool without three legs is just some sticks and a circle on the floor," said Dee-Dee, nodding. "Besides, Eugenia and I have different destinies—hers, a Parisian apartment; mine, captaining the high seas."

But Gertrude had already vanished into the void.

"I can't believe the lengths to which I must go," Eugenia said, climbing in after Gertrude.

Millicent emerged from the cocoon of her skirts and looked at Dee-Dee, the only Porch left in the room.

"They went into that tunnel, didn't they?" said Millicent.

Dee-Dee nodded.

"I can't believe the lengths to which I must go," Millicent sighed, then climbed in after Eugenia and Gertrude. "Dee-Dee, dear, will you hang by the door and replace the painting if anyone comes?"

Dee-Dee nodded and proceeded to climb up the door and hang from the top of it by her feet.

"Mind if I hang here?" she said.

"No problem," said the door.

Gertrude, Eugenia, and Millicent crawled through the dark tunnel toward the voices, until at last they reached the end, which was cordoned off by an ornate brass vent cover. Millicent, Gertrude, and Eugenia peered through the grate at the grisly scene unfolding on the other side.

There was a red haze. It was a room that could be described only as a "lair," outfitted in a style that could only be described as "vampire bordello": walls lined in crimson velvet, with a chandelier of wrought iron and black crystal, plush red couches, and floor lamps with sconces made of human skeletons.[1]

There were seven people milling about the room and chatting. They were wearing black velvet robes and red gloves. Their faces were obscured by porcelain masks in the shapes of various animals. This was a frightening sight, to be sure—grown people in porcelain animal masks are the stuff of nightmares. The barn owl and fox masks were especially terrifying—the bunny rabbit and proboscis monkey, somewhat less so. The one thing that almost ruined the effect of their spooky ensembles was their feet. Underneath the bottom hems of their robes, they wore normal adult stocking and socks and boots and shoes.

---

1   These were a popular home decor item during the Heyday of Mad Science, along with banisters made of femurs and drawer pulls made of scalpels. This was not, as you can imagine, a good idea.

"That's our dentist!" Eugenia hissed. "That's Dr. Luft! He wears socks with little bananas on them!"

Gertrude and Millicent gasped as the barn owl bent to scratch his ankles, which were indeed covered with tiny yellow knitted bananas.

"Our dentist is KRA!" Eugenia groaned, thinking of all the unwrapped mints she'd eaten from his candy jar.

Gertrude was shaken. If people as boring as Dr. Luft and as stiff as Mrs. Wintermacher were part of the KRA, which other trusted Antiquarian adults might be lurking under those masks?

But there was no time to wonder. The meeting was beginning.

"All kneel," said the one wearing the creepiest mask of all: a human face.

"Yes, dear leader," chorused the others.

The leader stood before an altar covered with dripping candles. Behind the altar was a velvet curtain with three big letters embroidered across it:

The leader pulled a cord and the curtain parted, revealing an oil portrait of a thin man with sharp cheeks, black eyes, and a maniacal smile, with pointed teeth shaped like upside-down triangles.

TALON SHARKTŪTH

The secret cohort sunk to their knees—rather creakily in the case of Dr. Luft—and raised their hands to the heavens.

"All hail Talon Sharktūth, Master of Life Eternal!"

This sent a cold sweat down Gertrude's hot spine.

Then the KRA began another soft chant, this time in another language. Gertrude and Millicent and Eugenia all exchanged uneasy glances, as all were thinking exactly the same thing: *Wow, these people can't sing very well.*

When the "song" came to its ragged, tentative conclusion, the leader kissed the oil portrait of Talon Sharktūth for what seemed to Gertrude like just a *little* too long, and just a *little* too close to the mouth.

"Very well. Now that we've begun, Member Five has updates about Operation OTV."

The masked miscreants clapped politely and sat cross-legged on the floor like kindergartners whilst Member Five paraded slowly, ceremonially, to the front of the room. Not a fly buzzed, not a drip dropped, not a breath breathed—even the second hand of the clock on the wall stiffened in the damp air as the fiendish figure pulled away her black hood and removed her porcelain rabbit mask. Underneath was none other than...

MRS. URSULA WINTERMACHER.

It was shocking enough to see their starchy etiquette teacher in this dark, cavernous, and illicit milieu, but more shocking still was what had apparently been lurking this whole time underneath her ornate hats: a clear plastic bathing cap labeled...

Dr Waters' Treatment for Chronic Lice
CAUTION—TOXIC

"I knew it!" Eugenia whispered. "I knew there was a problem under there!"

With some difficulty, Mrs. Wintermacher reached into a dark corner and pulled out a rolling green chalkboard filled with strange markings.

"Yes, thank you," she said, her voice shaking. "Thank you for allowing me the honor of continuing to seek full membership in your club. I have tried my very best as a junior member, and these have been the happiest days of my life."

The leader motioned for Mrs. Wintermacher to move along.

"Yes, of course. The Kyrgalops has reached full size. I drugged it with a tubful of chloroform and dragged it to an undisclosed location. The quandary of Operation OTV has been, of course, how to lure the creature to the desired location. But after spying on Millicent Quibb—wonderful idea, by the way—I believe I have figured out how to do it."

Mrs. Wintermacher paused for drama.

"It seems that the prized snack of the Kyrgalops is none other than our official town canine, the BICHON FRISE!"

"Aha!" the members exclaimed.

"Therefore," Mrs. Wintermacher said, "we must somehow amass all of the town's bichon frises into the desired location. The worm will bite through them and, in the process, perform its sacred task."

The leader ran her finger over the chin of her mask. "I'm listening...."

"So, I propose that we launch an operation to kidnap everyone's dogs in the middle of the night."

The leader hung her head and sighed. "Ugh. I don't know what to say. You're not very good at this. That is a dumb plan. The solution is simple. We get people to *bring* their dogs to *us*."

"Like, a dog donation drive?"

"No. Not a dog donation drive. A dog *show*. A dog beauty pageant. Tomorrow, at the desired location: at the Antiquarium Fairgrounds."

The masked KRA members gasped and nodded in agreement.

"My Gourd, she's good," murmured Dr. Luft. "But what will people think? Won't they blame us for their dogs being eaten by a giant worm?"

"Simple," said the leader. "We peg it on Millicent Quibb. The angry mob will take care of the rest."

Gertrude gasped and held her stomach. She pictured a pile of unsuspecting dogs torn into bloody pieces, bits of white fur flying, fluffy tails scattered to the wind like dandelion seeds—and Millicent tripping over her lab coat as she tried to outrun the angry mob. This, if nothing else, was cause for fainting.

"I will print up fliers," the leader said. "Members Three, Two, and One, you'll distribute them today. Then tomorrow, we will lure the worm to the desired location, where he will complete Operation OTV—"

"OPEN TALON'S VAULT!" Mrs. Wintermacher cried in ecstasy.

The leader gritted her teeth. "NOT. Out loud. We don't say it out loud. We say 'Operation OTV,' remember? In case we're being spied on?"

Now Gertrude was feeling even more faint. She found herself melting to the floor.

Millicent and Eugenia quickly caught Gertrude by her elbows, just in time to stop her body from thumping to the floor and making a terrible racket.

A close save, to be sure—but in diving to catch Gertrude, Millicent Quibb accidentally struck the middle toe of her left foot against the brass grate. She had no choice but to make that sound that you can't help but make when you stub your toe, which is something like:

"Oo—oo—oo—ooo—ow!—oo—yach!
—oo—ow ow ow ow ow!"

So much for silence.

The masked members of the KRA stiffened. "What was that?" whispered the leader. "Member Three, was that you? Did you stub your toe?"

Dr. Luft shook his barn owl mask. "Certainly not! You know I lost my toes in the war[2] and I overcompensate by wearing my banana socks!"

The evil cohort tiptoed toward the grate.

"Well, someone did," said the leader. Slowly, she pulled something brown and furry from her cloak and plodded toward the grate, where Millicent and her pupils clung to one another, praying for a way out.

"And that someone...

GETS THE STUB-RAT."

---

2 A skiing accident.

CHAPTER 14

TOWN HALL

I SEE SOMETHING moving over there, in the duct behind the heating vent!" said Dr. Luft.

The leader was calm. "Let the Stub-Rat deal with it."

Millicent and Eugenia were still trying desperately to smack Gertrude awake.

The Stub-Rat's sharp yellow fangs sparked along the floor as it paced toward the brass vent. It was a disturbing creature with ears like ragged moth wings and giant flared red nostrils that dripped with green snot.[1]

---

1 The Stub-Rat was bred in 1522 for the purposes of terrorizing children in a Dutch village. The children liked to sneak out at night to steal doughnuts from the doughnut store, stubbing their toes on the jutting cobblestones of the sidewalks as they went—then they'd be too tired the following morning to work their mandatory fourteen-hour shifts of plugging the dam with chewed bubblegum. So a Viologist named Geertgen Van Beerpgen bred a rat with razor teeth that could hear the sound of a stubbed toe from five miles away. When the children stubbed their toes while sneaking out to the doughnut store, the rat would scurry over and chew off their feet. Well, it worked: The Stub-Rat systematically chewed off all the children's feet, then the dam flooded and the village was wiped out. This is, of course, a cautionary tale against 1) child labor and hypocrisy, 2) breeding giant rats, and 3) placing civic trust in men named Geertgen Van Beerpgen. But I digress.

Millicent and Eugenia winced as the Stub-Rat fixed its homicidal gaze on the grate, its eyes glowing yellower and yellower, its wheezing growing wetter and wetter.

Just then, the familiar sound of a stub reverberated from the opposite corner of the lair:

"O o—o o—o o—o o o—o w!—o o—
yach!—oo—ow ow ow ow ow!"

The Stub-Rat stopped dead in its tracks and whipped its head around. The phantom stubber wailed again, and the Stub-Rat scampered to the other side of the room.

Grateful for the distraction, Millicent and Eugenia heaved Gertrude up the tunnel. The three collapsed in a heap on the floor of Mrs. Wintermacher's office, where they found Dee-Dee massaging her shoes.

"Sorry, stubbed my toes," she said calmly. "I was hanging from the top of the door by my feet and the wind blew it closed, several times. It was several stubs."

"RUN," whispered Millicent. And the four galloped away from Mrs. Wintermacher's school.

"Back so soon?" said Aunt Desdemona.

The Porches stumbled into the living room of the Parquette house. Their dresses were torn and their hair was wind-whipped from fleeing in the Gerbilcar.

"How was the lecture series at Miss Questions's?" said Uncle Ansel. "What was it on again?"

"Um...pens?" Gertrude was too distraught to think of something clever. Her ears were still ringing with the sounds of their ordeal: the scraping of the Stub-Rat's fangs; the screeching of the gerbil wheels as Millicent revved the motor for their quick escape; Mrs. Wintermacher's stinging words: "Open Talon Sharktūth's vault."

"This is a disaster!" Millicent had shouted from the open window of the racing Gerbilcar as they careened away. "They're going to use the Kyrgalops to bite through the entrance to Talon Sharktūth's vault! They want his monsters...his machines...his elixir!"

"What do we do?" Gertrude cried.

"We have no choice!" Millicent shouted into the wind. "Tomorrow we must go to the dog show and trap the Kyrgalops in midair!"

"How exactly will we do that?" Eugenia shouted.

"We'll fly over the contest in my aircraft, with the Prismuth cage hanging from the bottom. When the Kyrgalops crests over the trees, we will try to position ourselves so that it dives headfirst into the cage. I'll need all three of you to control the movement of the cage with dangling ropes.

But my aircraft is unwieldy, and there may be…loss of life. Canine, human…mine…"

Gertrude trembled. "Yours?"

"Well, if we fail, they will blame me, and murder me. If we succeed, they will still blame me, and murder me. Sigh. Such is the life of those who try to fix things—they often end up breaking themselves in the process. Oh well. Meet me at my house in the morning, nine AM."

And that is why, as Gertrude stood in the living room moments later, she could not come up with a better fake lecture topic than "pens."

But the family was too busy to notice. Aunt Desdemona and Uncle Ansel were polishing their collection of luxury paper clips, while the Lavinias chattered happily among themselves, braiding the bangs of their bichons. Only Lavinia-Steve looked up at her cousins, scanning their faces for some clue as to what was so obviously wrong.

Just then, Lavinia-Anne ran in from the street. "Mommy! You'll never guess what happened! I just over-heard some people talking—there's going to be a bichon frise beauty pageant tomorrow! We all have to bring our babies!"

The Lavinias shrieked and danced around the living room with their unsuspecting dogs.

Gertrude felt like she had just swallowed a gallon of scalding soup. "Um, I don't think that's such a good idea, you guys! Please, please don't do that!"

"Why not, Rude-Gert?" Uncle Ansel said.

"It's just, um, it's not—"

"She's worried that the dogs will get body dysmorphia if they're exposed to unrealistic standards of beauty," Eugenia said. "Come, Gertrude, I think you're tired from all those pens—let's go take a nap."

And the Porches hurried through the parlor and out the back door.

"You heard what Millicent said," Dee-Dee sighed. "We all need to gather our strength in our own way. I'm going to go read about sea captains, seeing as how I'm destined to be one."

"I'm going to break some rocks," said Eugenia. "What about you, Gert?"

"But...but...there has to be something we can do!" Gertrude said. "Can't we walk around and look for where Wintermacher is hiding the Kyrgalops?"

"It could be anywhere," said Eugenia.

"Some things cannot be fixed," Dee-Dee said.

"But, but...!" Gertrude was trying not to cry. "But the dogs! Millicent! Don't we have to try?"

Her sisters had no answers.

Gertrude thought of the ponytail-less dog statue in the center of town, and how tomorrow it wouldn't be just statues of dogs that lost their heads. What would Jacobus DeWeen, first mayor of Antiquarium, think of this mess?

DeWeen...DeWeen!

Gertrude got an idea.

"Um, sisters...I'm just going to um, walk around, I guess? To clear my head?"

But Gertrude was lying. Gertrude had other plans.

And as she walked through the back gate toward Main Street, determined to fix what couldn't be fixed, she had no idea that she was being...

FOLLOWED!

The office of Majestina DeWeen was located at the top of a marble staircase in the Town Hall of Antiquarium, and was guarded by a line of secretaries, ten in all.

Gertrude's heart rattled the buttons on her Taffetteen as she curtsied to the tenth secretary. "Good day to you. I was hoping to see the mayor?"

The secretary peered at Gertrude with a raised eyebrow. Her dress was covered in filth, and her hair had been whipped into a froth by the wind. "Ohhh, I see, you're one of the orphans. Let me see if I can grab the mayor. One minute."

The tenth secretary whispered to the ninth, who whispered to the eighth, and so on, until finally the first secretary silently beckoned her to the door of the mayor.

Inside the office was a group of orphans in tattered rags. Majestina, dripping in red Taffetteen, was singing into a microphone.

> *Though you have no parents*
> *You will always be*
> *Welcome in our little town*
> *Courtesy of me*
>
> *I will give you blankets*
> *I'll give you croissants*
> *I will give you better clothes*
> *To silence children's taunts*
>
> *Kindness costs you nothing*
> *Kindness is for free*
> *So please take my donation*
> *And always think of me!*

"I love you all, each one," she said, then held up a large paper check in the amount of one dollar, while photographers clicked their flashbulbs.[2]

When the orphans had gone, the mayor sank back into her official chair, then pulled a bowl of dark cherries from her desk drawer and began to eat.

From the doorway, Gertrude cleared her throat.

"Ahhh!" Majestina screamed.

Gertrude emerged from the shadowy corner. "Sss... sss...sssorry," she whispered, barely able to form a word. It was MAJESTINA DEWEEN. There was no one in all of Antiquarium as grand as Majestina DeWeen!

"You scared me, I thought all the orphans had gone! Come out from the shadows, dear," Majestina said, biting into a cherry. "Thaaaaat's it. Can you tell me your name?"

"Grootude," Gertrude said, trying to make her mouth cooperate. "I mean, Bertrode. I mean, Gertfood...oh, never mind. And I'm actually not an orphan, although, I guess actually I am?" She pressed her lips together to stop herself from oversharing any further.

---

2 Now, every dollar counts, and a donation of any size to a charitable organization is a beautiful thing, but as the sum total of Majestina DeWeen's wealth was approximately eighteen million dollars, a one-dollar donation seemed to not really warrant a song, a giant check, and a roomful of photographers. But I digress.

"You're funny," said Majestina, handing Gertrude a cherry. "I like that. Now, how can your mayor help you today?"

"Yes, well..." Gertrude took a deep breath. "I actually just wanted to tell you something, um...bad?"

Have you ever had to tell something troublesome to a powerful adult? You know how it's one of the scariest things you could do, right up there with trying to step on a cockroach? Because even if what you're saying is true, the powerful adult might not believe you, and you just have a vague sense that somehow you might end up getting in even more trouble because you bothered to speak up in the first place? I hate that. Anyhow, this is exactly how Gertrude felt.

Majestina squinted. "Go on, plum-pie...."

"Um, so, you know how there's that upcoming contest for bichon frises?"

"My gourd, I LOVE that idea. I wish I'd thought of it myself! Won't that be the most fabulous thing you ever saw in your whole *life*?"

"Yes, certainly, and I love dogs and animals and bugs and all creatures of earth more than anything, but...well, it's hard to explain why, but I think you should actually, um, cancel the contest."

Majestina giggled. "Well now, why would I do that? Do you...hate dogs?"

"No! It's just, well, the dogs are in danger. Of being... eaten."

The mayor's fabulous eyebrows floated toward her hair. "*Eaten*? Eaten by what, exactly, potato-puff?"

Gertrude started to panic. Her mind went fuzzy, and when her mind went fuzzy, her mouth took over. "Well, there seems to be some kind of giant worm on the loose? And these bad guys are basically trying to open a vault, and they're using the bichons to get the worm to bite through it, and so you have to cancel the contest to save the dogs! And we're going to try to trap the worm with the Prismuth cage we made, but it might not work, and then the dogs will be dead and my teacher will be murdered and my life will be over and it's too sad to even be comprehended!"

Majestina's eyebrows went flat. "Wow," she said. "That's quite a tale. Let me see what I can do about that."

Suddenly Majestina's secretary appeared in the doorway. "Ms. Mayoress? Call for you on line two."

Gertrude beamed as Majestina disappeared into the next room. It worked! Majestina was going to cancel the contest! Gertrude looked at her toes and smiled, knocking them together. *Nice work, old chap!* she thought. *They told you it couldn't be done, but you did it! You and your big ideas saved the day!*

Majestina reappeared a moment later wearing a frown. "Bad news, pickle-pie. It seems like you might be in some trouble at home. You're going to have to wait in the hallway because...

YOUR AUNT AND UNCLE ARE COMING TO GET YOU."

CHAPTER 15

THE BAD PART

THIS IS THE PART of the book where the main character—what one's English teacher might call the *protagonist*, before brushing chalk off the arm of their sweater and taking a deep breath in a way that suggests that their dishwasher broke that morning—is sunk. Down in the dumps. Has lost everything. I've chosen to feature Gertrude as the protagonist of this story, though any of the Porches or Millicent could have been a very fine protagonist; I just happen to know Gertrude a little better in real life, which makes it easier to speculate about what the protagonist is feeling and wanting and losing and gaining and all those things that protagonists have to do. It's not easy to be the protagonist, because you are the one who has to feel the most, and ugh, who has the energy?

Anyway, there comes a time when the protagonist has lost it all. It's not fun to write, and it's not fun to read. Someone you hopefully have come to care about or perhaps relate to in some way is in pain and probably alone and doesn't know what to do next. Maybe it reminds you of a time when you felt that way too.[1]

In any case, Gertrude's rock bottom involved being trapped as well—not in a basement like I was, but in a small turret[2] at the top of a winding staircase in the attic of Aunt Desdemona and Uncle Ansel's house.

Gertrude had been sitting on the floor of the turret[3] since yesterday afternoon, when Aunt Desdemona had collected her from Town Hall. "Lavinia-Steve has told me *everything*," she'd said. "About how Marjory Questions told you to steal my brooches. And how she followed you to the mayor's office—and then I call there and I find out that you're ranting about canceling the dog contest? Why? Why would anyone try to cancel a dog contest?"

---

1 I know it does for me: I am reminded of the time when I accidentally locked myself in the basement of my house and had to stay there for eight weeks and survived on the one thing I buy in bulk and keep in the basement, which is string cheese. I had hypothermia and diarrhea. After eight weeks, I realized that the key to the basement door was in my hair.

2 "Turret" is a slightly more succinct way of saying "small tower." Why not just say "small tower" and omit the long footnote? I don't know. Next time I'll just say "small tower," I PROMISE.

3 Gahhh, I've done it again! I'm sorry. Next time. Small tower.

Lavinia-Steve could be heard weeping softly in the background the entire time.

Eugenia said it best: "Once a Lavinia, always a Lavinia."

"You are a menace to all bichon-kind," Uncle Ansel had said. "There's no way you're going to the dog contest, and there's no way you're going back to Marjory Questions, whoever she is. How was the mayor's office furniture, by the way? Gorgeous?"

Grantie Lettuce had turned her head in slow little jerks, like a sputtering sprinkler. "I smelled a Silly Sally." There was something like triumph behind her long, milky stare.

Gertrude had awoken that morning in the turret,[4] knowing that the contest was starting soon. Her face was puffy from crying, and her mouth was dry. She thought she might have dreamt the whole torturous sequence of events—but there she was, still trapped in the cold tower, sandwiched between Uncle Ansel's collection of snakeskin belts and a colony of sleeping brown bats hanging from the rafters.

Aunt Desdemona had locked Eugenia and Dee-Dee in their garden shed in the back, and they were screaming and pounding on the doors, to no avail. This was all her fault—as usual.

---

4 Gahhhhh! What am I DOING???

Gertrude thought of Millicent, who at that moment was probably waiting on her front porch, tapping her toe and checking her watch and wondering, *Where are they?! I can't trap this worm by myself!* Probably she would be jumping at each rustle in the bushes, crestfallen each time a chipmunk emerged instead of her new pupils. *I guess they didn't like me after all*, she would think, wondering if it was the worm guts on her boots that did it, or the worm guts in her hair, or just the whole package.

Gertrude even thought of the Kyrgalops, barreling toward the cluster of little bichons. The worm would just be trying to get a bite of its favorite snack, oblivious to the consequences. It was merely hungry, an orphan, a pawn in the KRA's plot. After the deed was done, they would probably murder it and dump it in a ditch. This caused Gertrude to curl into a ball on the floor. What would the look in its eyes be as it realized that Mrs. Wintermacher, who had fed and cared for it, was just using it, and was now through? *What did I do wrong?* it would wonder.

I told you: a bummer!

Gertrude peered through the tiny window of the SMALL TOWER.[5] To her great dismay, Aunt Desdemona, Uncle Ansel, the seven Lavinias and their seven

---

5 Happy? Do you miss *turret* now?

bichon frises were marching proudly out the door, each dog adorned with a different-color headband. They had no idea that they were walking right into a worm trap!

Lavinia-Steve looked up at Gertrude, her eyes red from weeping.

"Don't go!" Gertrude cried out the window.

But none of them heard her.

Everything had gone wrong, despite her best efforts. Dogs would perish, evil would triumph, Millicent would be blamed, and everything good would be over.

It's my fault, she thought. *Me and my big ideas. I'm just foolish. Foolish to think that Majestina DeWeen would believe me. Foolish to think I could keep my sisters safe. Foolish to believe that my mother was a nice woman named Pookie who farmed garlic, foolish to believe that anyone ever really wanted me.*

See what I mean? No one wants to read this, it's such a bummer. And yet it's how she felt. Have you ever felt something like this? Gertrude felt very alone in that moment, but was unaware that one day someone might read her tale and might feel similarly. So really she wasn't alone, though there was no way of knowing that at the time.

She looked out the window again, at the shed where Eugenia and Dee-Dee were trapped. Through the dusty window she could see their frightened faces.

Gertrude had to send them a message, in the event that

the worm made its way from the fairgrounds and ate them all. In the dust of her window, she wrote a message:

Inside the shed, Eugenia and Dee-Dee squinted at the message. Then Dee-Dee raised her finger to the dust and drew a message of her own.

Well.

At least, in the darkness, there was still the greatest of life's offerings: little sisters.

Eugenia raised her finger to the window and made some additional markings to the heart.

Hmm, a bat? I wonder what she means, Gertrude thought, looking overhead at the bats as they napped in the rafters of the small tower. *It was a bat that got us into this whole gigantic dill pickle in the first place, when you think about it. Oh, why did I have to bring a Bat Straightener to school? Why do I have to have such big, weird ideas? I mean, it was honestly kind of a good idea, even though it got us all expelled.*

Gertrude chuckled to herself as she waved hello to the bats. They had awakened from their nap, and they looked hungry.

She pulled a bunch of figs from her pocket that Aunt Desdemona had given her for dinner, figs that she'd been too distraught to eat.

"Bottoms up, kids," she said.

The bats looked around as if to say, "Who, us?"

"Yeah, you," Gertrude said with a laugh. They fluttered down to Gertrude. They sat on her knees and on her shoulders and on the top of her head, and they munched on the soft purple fruit.

They really were a beautiful sight. All creatures are, if you think about it.

Beneath the figs, something else was still lurking in her pocket. The Bat Straightener. She pulled the vest over her dress. *I could hook up to all these bats and they could fly me out of here!*

Imagine? That would be funny.

There was still one big bat harness attached to the end of the rope. Then, as if he understood that she needed help, one bat opened his wings, and Gertrude gently slid the straps of the bat harness over them. Then another, then another—until all the bats were strapped in, back to front.

Then they flapped in unison, their wings working in tandem, like a team of rowers, and Gertrude was lifted off the ground.

"Whoooaaaa there, little fellas!"

But the bats did not stop flapping. They flapped higher and higher. Then they flapped out the window, dragging Gertrude over the ledge and into the open air.

She looked down at the ground four stories below and imagined plummeting onto the barbed wrought iron gate, or into the pile of broken porcelain from the third-floor bathroom renovation—but the bats flapped as hard as they could, swooshing in unison, and Gertrude floated gently to the ground.

She wept at how amazing it was, the generosity of the bats. She freed the bats from the harness and kissed each one on the soft brown fur atop their heads before they flapped away, bellies full of figs. She could see the bones and muscles working inside the leathery brown wings, pumping, soaring, and she thought: Every creature, no matter how bizarre, or reviled, has a place.

And what was her place?

To help, or at least try.

To love the world, and treat it with tenderness.

To marvel at what is, while it still is.

She ran to the garden shed where Eugenia and Dee-Dee were being held captive and smacked the padlock off the door with an old iron pipe.

Eugenia and Dee-Dee emerged to find their older sister standing there, looking like some kind of hero.

Eugenia hugged her—quickly, but tightly, and with purpose.

Dee-Dee tipped her cowboy hat and winked. "Today is a big day for you," she said. And though Gertrude didn't know exactly what Dee-Dee meant, as usual, she could feel that it somehow might be true.

Just then, there was a humming overhead, like a thousand mosquitos. Through the din rang a majestic voice from the sky, the voice of Millicent Quibb: "Girls!" she cried.

"WE'RE LATE FOR THE PAGEANT!"

CHAPTER 16

THE PROBLEM WITH THE POOL

THE PORCHES CLUNG to Millicent as they soared through the air on the back of her aircraft. It was a sort of flying motorcycle in the shape of a housefly, with an abdomen of bolted black steel and translucent wings that were made of, ironically enough, flyswatters. The Prismuth cage dangled below, catching on the tops of oaks and pines as they buzzed past.

"Please forgive the state of my Flycycle!" Millicent screamed into the whipping wind. "I know it needs a good vacuuming, but there was no time to waste!" Millicent reached into her side bag and handed the Porches their lab coats. "Here! You'll need these!"

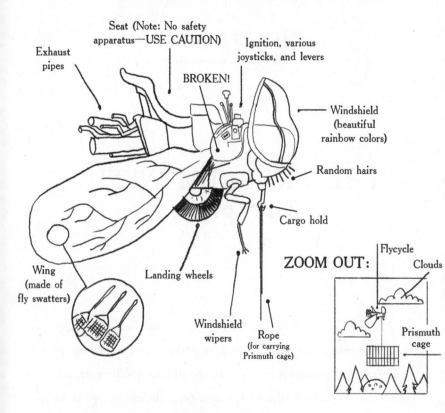

"I'm sorry we didn't come this morning—we were trapped!" screamed Gertrude.

"I figured!" Millicent shouted through the swirling air. "Well, first I thought that you had abandoned me and hated me! Then I wondered if perhaps something had gone wrong and you didn't completely hate me after all! So I thought I'd come see for myself!"

"I went to see the mayor! I made it worse!" Gertrude shouted into the wind.

"I know! It's okay!" Millicent shouted back.

And that was that.

Gertrude was petrified of falling off, of course—Flycycles lack seatbelts and other general safety features—but she allowed herself to unsqueeze her eyes just long enough to look down on the whole of Antiquarium.

Look at me. I am actually flying, she thought, and smiled wide to greet the sky. For how often can a young person say that about themselves?

But this was no time for wonder. There were dogs to rescue, vaults to keep locked, towns to save.

A moment later, the Antiquarium Fairgrounds came into view over a battalion of pine trees. An emerald Ferris wheel kissed the clouds. A cerulean swimming pool rippled gently in the warm breeze. A brass marching band beat their drums and blew their tubas as they weaved through the cheering crowd. A bandstand was flanked by rolling flags bearing the town bird of Antiquarium, the white dove.[1]

Millicent turned to her pupils. "I'm going to land in that forsythia bush across the street. I've piloted this Flycycle dozens of times but have never once landed it without a major accident. I'm sure it will be fine, right?"

---

1 The technical term for this bird, bred specifically to look fancy when let out of boxes at weddings, is "the albino release pigeon."

The Porch sisters were still picking forsythia buds and branches from their hair and pants when the marching band played its final note, at which time the boys banging the bass drums all took it upon themselves to do long, mismatched solos.

Gertrude surveyed the scene through the branches of forsythia: hundreds of Antiquarians shouting gaily, packed like pickles around the bandstand, and next to it...

THE DOG SHOW RING...

...a circular pen surrounded by a high wrought iron gate. The bars were just far apart enough that you could watch a dog beauty pageant through them, but just close enough to prevent the contestants from escaping, should a giant dog-eating worm happen to crash the party.

Suddenly, the crowd erupted into thunderous applause as Majestina DeWeen took the stage. She wore a long, luxurious overcoat of white fluff so reminiscent of a bichon frise that one had to wonder if the coat was perhaps, in fact, made of them.

"I know, isn't it fabulous!" she said, running her hands

over her coat while the crowd roared. "When at a dog show, dress as the dogs do, yes?!"

The crowd laughed at their glamorous mayor. Gertrude hung her head. Why didn't Majestina believe her?

"Thank you all for coming to this fabulous affair, organized by the Bichon Frise Enthusiast Club of Antiquarium. They asked if I'd emcee—and how could I say no to my favorite dogs that happen also to be the only dogs allowed in Antiquarium? Why, I love them so much, I'm wearing them!"

The crowd laughed nervously.

"Kidding! Obviously! No bichon frises were harmed in the making of this gorgeous garment!"

"Maltipoos, on the other hand...," said Eugenia.

"We're going to get started soon, so would all our canine contestants and their handlers please enter our show ring here...?"

The Porches watched in horror as the thirty or so contestants, Aunt Desdemona and the seven Lavinias and their seven bichons among them, filed happily into the pen, whereupon Ashley Cookie, Esq., closed the gate and fixed it with a heavy iron padlock.

"I can't believe we're going to all this trouble to save the Lavinias' dogs," Eugenia griped, though of course she knew that they were also going to the trouble of saving the Lavinias, and the rest of the town besides.

Lavinia-Steve clutched her bichon and looked around in bewilderment, sensing that something was not right inside that pen. Why, for instance, did a show ring need to be padlocked shut?

"Alright," Millicent said, "let's load up the Flycycle. Pupeels, get ready to man your ropes. We must be ready with our Prismuth cage at a moment's notice."

Dee-Dee was distracted by a rustling behind her, and she turned to find a black-cloaked figure hauling her Prismuth cage toward the swimming pool.

"Stop!" Dee-Dee cried. "My baby! My rainbow baby!"

The cloaked figure's hood blew off, and Gertrude saw a clear plastic bathing cap underneath—DR. WATERS' CHRONIC LICE TREATMENTS—CAUTION—TOXIC—and knew in an instant who had run off with the cage:

It was of course

None other than

You guessed it

Say it with me

All together now

Three

Two

One

MRS. WINTERMACHER

Member Number Five hurled the Prismuth cage into the pool and laughed maniacally as the cage sank to the bottom.

Gertrude paused to consider her joke. What was so funny? Why would Millicent and her pupils be thwarted by having to pull a featherlight cage from the bottom of a pool that was only three feet deep?

But then...why was Millicent sinking to the ground and screaming "Noooooooooooooo!"?

Gertrude thought maybe she was being sarcastic—but then Eugenia did the same, banging her fists on the sidewalk and crying. Even Dee-Dee, who had never been angry in her life, clutched her cowboy hat to her chest and screamed in agony. What was Gertrude missing? She stared pleadingly at Mrs. Wintermacher.

"Chlorine! Hahahahahaha!"

Gertrude was still lost. "Yes, but, um, what about it?"

"Look at your precious cage, in the chlorine!"

Gertrude watched as the strong right angles of the Prismuth rectangle caved listlessly into a limp pile on the bottom of the pool.

"Chlorine makes Prismuth as limp as spaghetti! Remember?"

Now, if you'll recall, earlier I *did* mention that chlorine changes the molecular structure of Prismuth and makes it ultra-malleable. (See page 147 if you don't believe me.) How malleable, exactly? Though it doesn't sound very technical, Prismuth soaked in chlorine has the exact malleability of cooked spaghetti.

This is the tragic flaw of a Prismuth cage: Any run-of-the-mill municipal pool could spell its instant demise.

"I did my research on Prismuth last night," said Mrs. Wintermacher. "After I heard you'd be here with a Prismuth cage."

Gertrude stiffened. "Who told you that?"

"My friend Majesti—" Mrs. Wintermacher stopped herself. "I mean, my friend Susan."

Gertrude's knees buckled.

She had told Majestina about their plan to trap the Kyrgalops with a Prismuth cage.

And Majestina had told Mrs. Wintermacher.

And Mrs. Wintermacher was part of the KRA.

Did that mean…could it mean…that Majestina DeWeen was…was…?

There was almost an audible whoosh: the sound of the bottom falling out of the world.

She stumbled through the crowd to the edge of the bandstand, where Majestina DeWeen was belting a big-band number:

> *Tiny little dogs*
> *White and fluffy dogs*
> *Thank gourdness they're not bats or cats*
> *Or rats or mice or frogs*
>
> *We love their perfect fur*
> *Whiter than a dove*
> *Trim them like a topiary*
> *Shower them with love*
>
> *And shampoooooooo….*

Gertrude stopped at the lip of the stage.

"STOP! THE! CONTEST!" she bellowed.

The crowd went silent. Majestina stared down at Gertrude, her eyebrows flat as the horizon. She smiled and waved her finger back and forth.

"Now, now. Don't be a Silly Sally."

Gertrude knitted her brow. *I thought that was just something Grantie Lettuce says.*

Gertrude was about to shout again when there came a scream from the crowd.

Then another.

Then another.

Then the frantic clacking of heels.

Then the frantic barking of dogs.

Then the frantic wailing of Antiquarians—

Then a roar.

THE KYRGALOPS HAD ARRIVED.

CHAPTER 17

THE BATTLE

THE MONSTROUS HEAD of the Kyrgalops crested over the perimeter of pines. Its four eyes glowed yellow. Its mouth was wide as a giant cauldron, with several concentric circles of gnashing teeth that got smaller and smaller until they vanished into a viscous red abyss of gullet and guts.

Inside the padlocked show ring, Aunt Desdemona huddled the Lavinias and their seven bichons under her arms and wept.

Lavinia-Steve put her arm through the bars of the gate and tugged on Gertrude's sleeve. Her eyes were bloodshot, her stress-sneezes were constant.

"I'm sorry, Gertrude—achoo!—I was confused—achoo! I thought it was cool that you got to go to a different school 'cause I actually kind of hate Mrs. Wintermacher and the other Lavinias are kind of mean to me and I just wanted to know what you guys were doing 'cause it looked fun but then Eugenia told me to go away and I felt left out—aaaaaachooo!—and then I saw you stealing the brooches and sneaking into Town Hall and I told on you because I was sort of jealous I think! But now there's a giant worm! Did your school, like, make the worm, or...?"

"No!" Gertrude said. "Someone else did! But we're trying to trap it!"

"Oh my gourd, that's crazy! Achoo! Can I help?"

And in that moment, Gertrude forgave Lavinia-Steve for being an eavesdropper and a tattletale. She had her sisters, forever and always, and Lavinia-Steve seemed to have no one.

Meanwhile, the Kyrgalops turned its attention toward the gated pen, which was stuffed with people and bichons.

"Help us, Gertrude!" cried Aunt Desdemona.

"Hold tight!" Gertrude cried. "I'm going to get you out of here!"

But Gertrude didn't see anything that she could use to break the padlock off the gate.

She fished inside the pocket of her lab coat and felt something: a tiny bag filled with Rapier Vine seeds that had been sitting there since the pizza party. This got her to thinking: Might a delicate spray of Rapier Vines be able to crack the iron of the padlock, as they had cracked Millicent's chandelier after growing out of Dee-Dee's mouth? There was only one way to find out.

Gertrude swallowed the whole packet of seeds.

The vines began to spill forth from her mouth, and she pointed them toward the iron padlock.

Aunt Desdemona and the Lavinias all watched in horror—all except for Lavinia-Steve, whose horror was tinged with wonder.

The Rapier Vines invaded the nooks and crannies in and around the padlock, and before long, the iron behemoth cracked in two. Dee-Dee rushed over and poured a glass of lemonade from a nearby stand down Gertrude's gullet, and the vines withered away.

"What...was that?" Lavinia-Steve asked.

"It was basically mad science!" Gertrude grinned. "You should try it sometime!"

The crowd of bichon frises burst forth from the pen and scattered onto the field. The worm exploded over the tops of the pines and flopped onto the fairgrounds. It stood taller than the Ferris wheel.

The Kyrgalops surveyed the scene with its four eyes,[1] not sure where it wanted to chomp first.

---

1 And yes, the eyes were crossed.

Amidst all the chaos, Millicent Quibb stood still, with her eyes closed. "It's all fine," she mumbled to herself. "I'm doing a good job. Maybe if I open my eyes, the worm will be gone or dead. Should I try?"

Millicent opened one eye.

"Nope. Still there."

Then Millicent got an idea.

"Eureka!"

She ran to the stage, where Majestina DeWeen was cowering behind some trumpet players, and pulled the white fluffy coat from the mayor's luxurious frame.

Millicent tossed the coat over her back and ran onto the lawn, where the bichons were running around like frightened, well...bichons.

"Woof, woof!" she hollered. "Do you see me, Kyrgalops?! I'm the biggest bichon of all! Ruff, ruff!"

The worm trained its four crossed eyes on the large, deformed dog that was malingering in the center. It followed her for a moment, then decided that this big dog, which was zigzagging and making bizarre, unearthly shrieks, was perhaps not the dog it wanted to eat, because it looked diseased, and so it slithered off in search of more robust snacks.

Majestina DeWeen, now coatless, her raven hair wild and out of place, stumbled to the microphone at the front of the stage.

"Listen well, my town, and I will tell you why this terror has befallen us! The infamous mad scientist MILLICENT QUIBB is in our midst! I didn't think it was possible, I didn't think she was real, but she's here, and she's trying to destroy us!"

The crowd stopped dead in their tracks, even as the worm continued to flop around on the grass.

"Clearly, this worm is her creation!"

The crowd craned their necks to see the infamous, legendary, probably-not-real-but-who-else-could-possibly-be-responsible-for-this-worm-situation MAD SCIENTIST. Having someone to blame gave them strength and confidence.

"She broke our statue!" Ashley Cookie, Esq., cried.

"She made my store smell like meat!" Mme Flambé cried.

"She stole my socks!" cried Dr. Luft.

"Yes, it was she who brought this scourge upon us!" Majestina cried. "And look—there she is, trying to lure her monster onto the field so that it eats us all!"

Millicent was still zigzagging and screaming. It was not clear whether she was trying to lure the monster or was simply having an aneurism, but the crowd spotted her immediately. The men brandished fancy writing pens from their briefcases, the women brandished the points of their parasols! They had to do *something*! They converged en masse at the center of the field. They were going to skewer Millicent like a kebab!

Dee-Dee and Eugenia watched as the angry mob closed in on their teacher. "Ugh, now we have to go save Millicent!" Eugenia said.

She thought fast, remembering her invisible rock stashed in her pocket—the one she'd stolen from the mad science library. She cracked the rock into dozens of invisible pieces, then fumbled around the invisible pile and handed piece after invisible piece to Dee-Dee, who used her catapult to launch them in the direction of the crowd, where they bonked people on top of the head.

"What has bonked me?" one man cried.

"She's using mad science to bonk us!" cried another.

The crowd backed away from the hailstorm of invisible rocks, leaving just enough room for Eugenia and Dee-Dee to run in and drag Millicent from the melee.

"Excellent mad science improvisation," Millicent sputtered. She hugged the children brusquely, then sprinted away from the fairgrounds as fast as she could, off to Gourd-Knows-Where.

After nursing the bumps on their heads, the bewildered crowd turned their attention to Eugenia and Dee-Dee. Luckily, the children had an exit strategy: They mounted the sturdy Flycycle, which lay mangled beyond the forsythia bushes, and buzzed into the air. The crowd watched with fury as the adolescent etiquette-school rejects sailed off into the clouds aboard a giant fly.

Gertrude sighed with relief as Dee-Dee and Eugenia flew to safety, but then she remembered her other problem: the Kyrgalops. The hungry worm hoovered one rogue bichon into its horrifying rotating mouth parts, then another.

I don't know what to do! Gertrude thought. *I'm out of big ideas!*

Mrs. Wintermacher was holding up a bichon frise as a treat, trying to lure the worm toward the opening of the vault, but the Kyrgalops had turned its attention to the dense crowd of Antiquarians. It swerved past the pool where the Prismuth cage floated, limp as spaghetti.

Spaghetti.

Spaghetti—could not spaghetti be used to make a lasso? Had she not made a rather successful spaghetti lasso just nights before?

She waded into the pool and retrieved the bars of the Prismuth cage, which were now light and bendy as noodles.

Waist high in water, she tied the ends of the Prismuth ropes together, then emerged with a long lasso.

She stood behind the Kyrgalops and whistled to get its attention.

"Hey, wormie!" she cried.

The Kyrgalops didn't turn around—but the angry mob did. They saw Gertrude standing in the pool, soaking like a drowned rat and holding a long, glimmering rope of rainbow crystals. She had to make it quick, before the crowd pounced.

She remembered the lessons of the lemons and the tutelage of the tunnel: If you wish to make a worm come toward you, just sing to it in a low voice. She cleared her throat and sang as low and loud as she could:

> *Hey there, Kyrgalops,*
> *I think you're the tops!*
> *You ate a dog, but it's okay*
> *You didn't ask to be this way....*

The Kyrgalops turned toward Gertrude and she launched the Prismuth lasso, which landed around the worm's thick neck. The worm smiled maniacally at Gertrude—eyes crossed, mouth whirling, ready to pounce.

Just then, something strange happened.

Slowly, the Kyrgalops closed its eyes and bowed. It pressed its slimy crimson forehead to Gertrude's, and then, quite improbably, it began...

to purr...

Could it be? Yes, it was! The purring sounded more like a chainsaw than a kitten, but still.

The crowd watched in stunned silence.

Gertrude breathed in the closeness of the Kyrgalops: the feeling of the rough scales; the coolness of the slime; the purr that rattled her bones and blew out her eardrums; the smell, which was, oddly enough, not unlike the smell of old soda. "Hello," she whispered.

Why did the Kyrgalops bow to her? How could it know that she was a friend?

These, and other mysteries, are beyond the scope of this book.

Gertrude climbed atop the Kyrgalops's back, holding the Prismuth lasso like a set of reins, and nudged the worm lightly with her heels.

Nothing happened. The worm wouldn't move. That is, until she did as she'd been trained, and wailed the highest note she possibly could—THE BEST AND SOME-TIMES ONLY WAY to make worms run in the opposite direction.

Passersby scattered and screamed as Gertrude steered the worm down Pantsville Avenue, up DeWeen Boulevard, and over the sands of Red Dune Beach, where the Kyrgalops dove happily into the water.

Gertrude let go of the reins and bobbed in the rough

surf, tossing to and fro, while the Kyrgalops disappeared into the sea.

The waves were rough, and Gertrude's wet lab coat was heavy. She paddled and writhed and struggled to stay afloat as the waves pummeled her from overhead. She was a long way from the shore, and her legs were getting tired, until she heard a whirring from on high.

She looked up: The Flycycle was hovering above. Dee-Dee was captaining the vessel while Eugenia clung to her back.

"Hold on!" Eugenia cried, lowering a rope from the side of the Flycycle.

Gertrude hoisted herself onto the back of the airship.

Dee-Dee was trying to contain a certain explosive giddiness beneath her usual fortress of calm. "Gertrude. I don't know if you can see what's going on right now, but I am living out my destiny: I am being a sea captain!"

Indeed: There was her tiny little sister, the stalwart captain of a straight and sturdy vessel, soaring over the sea.

Gertrude smiled and patted her on the back. "That's wonderful, Deed."

"How did you tame the worm?" Eugenia asked. "That was probably the most impressive thing I've ever seen, and you know how hard it is for me to say things like that."

"I don't know," Gertrude said. She knew that she had beckoned it to her with her low baritone—but that didn't

explain why the worm had become so docile, so tender.

"Well, whatever it was, it rocked."

And Gertrude wrapped her arms around her little sisters and sniffed deeply, wanting to remember this moment forever, and knowing that smell was the best way to do it. There was only one thing missing.

"By the way," she asked, "where is Millicent?"

Dee-Dee piloted the Flycycle over the towering waves, then spoke the most harrowing words that had ever left her lips:

"MILLICENT IS GONE."

CHAPTER 18

THE END

THEY MET IN SECRET.

The leader lit the candles. The loyal members of the evil organization were sweating beneath their awful animal masks. Something bad was about to happen. They gripped the couch cushions and the chair handles and their knees and anything else they could find, bracing for the worst.

"Well," sighed the leader. "That was...something."

A tense silence. The sound of Dr. Luft scratching the banana sock on his ankle was as loud as a meteor ripping through the atmosphere.

"Obviously, we failed to open Talon Sharktūth's vault," the leader said matter-of-factly. "Luckily, as planned, we have pawned our PR problem onto Millicent Quibb, who seems to have fled. As for those children, I'm sure Desdemona and Ansel can keep them in line until the time comes."

The group nodded.

"And as for you, Member Five..."

Mrs. Wintermacher perked up.

"You are banished from the organization. And from Antiquarium, obviously. Your handling of the simple tasks associated with this all-important mission was so poor that we *should* kill you—but we've decided to let you live. So. You can leave town now."

Mrs. Wintermacher stood with her jaw open.

"Oh, I meant that you can leave town *right* now," said the leader. "Was that not clear? My apologies. The no-murder offer expires in...ten minutes."

Mrs. Wintermacher laid her cape on the tufted red leather sofa. "It was so nice to get to know all of you."

The group said nothing as she moped away from the hidden lair, dragging her huge hat behind her.

"Well, now that the weakest link has been eliminated, we will forge ahead with our plans. I just need to regroup first. You're all dismissed."

The remaining members filed out, leaving their animal masks and capes on wall hooks near the door, until the leader was alone.

She slumped over to a mirror on the back of the door.

She pried her porcelain mask from the pruned flesh under-neath and stared at her reflection. "I am coming, Talon! Wait for me, my prince! We shall be together...forever!"

If the Porch Sisters had been there, if they had seen who was behind the mask, it would have saved the pupils of the Millicent Quibb School of Etiquette for Young Ladies of Mad Science a lot of trouble.

But as it was, the trouble was just beginning.

On a velvet fainting couch in the Parquette parlor, Aunt Desdemona executed a flawless Upright Sit with Straight Back. Across from her sat the Porch Sisters, who were still soaking wet from having crashed the Flycycle into the town fountain.

Ashley Cookie, Esq., had dragged the children back to Aunt Desdemona's house and shoved them through the front door, shouting: "*You* deal with this!"

And so Aunt Desdemona was dealing with it, shaken as she was by the day's events. "Porch children. Your crimes are as follows: 1) falsifying an etiquette school, 2) associat-ing with a mad scientist, and lastly and most importantly, 3) creating a giant worm monster and releasing it upon the town."

"We wish we could take credit, dear Aunt," Dee-Dee sighed, "but the worm was a creation of the KRA. And Fifi Bubblegumme, of course."

"You keep saying 'KRA' and 'Fifi Bubblegumme,' and I keep not knowing what those are, so just shush and let me continue!" Aunt Desdemona clutched her pearl necklace with one hand and her pearl brooch with another. "For your crimes, we are sending you all to Austria, where we should have sent you from the start. We were being cheap, and that's what happens when you're cheap." Aunt Desdemona threw a look at Uncle Ansel, who burst into tears.

"Why don't you just leave us on a Parisian sidewalk and forget that we ever existed?" Eugenia snarled. "Why must you control our every movement?"

"Because we are being paid handsomely to watch you until you are of age!" Aunt Desdemona blurted out, then immediately covered her mouth. Grantie Lettuce raised an eyebrow at Aunt Desdemona. "I mean…I simply meant that we are being paid…in *grace*, from our good gourd above. And we simply cannot do without our…grace. Anyway, off to Austria you go. Do you have anything else to say for yourselves?"

Gertrude wanted to say something, but she knew it would make the Parquettes mad. Then again, her mouth was already moving.

"I actually would like to say, um...," Gertrude began softly.

"Yes? Out with it, Rude-Gert!"

Gertrude took a deep breath. Even though everything had gone topsy-turvy, deep in her heart, she knew something about herself that she didn't know before: She truly valued certain things—things like...truth! Caring for animals! Caring for people! And the people she knew who valued those things too, well...they seemed to like her just fine. Her sisters liked her. Lavinia-Steve seemed to tentatively like her. Millicent Quibb liked her. Even a Kyrgalops liked her! A Kyrgalops, who was built to chew through solid steel, had bowed to her and purred like a kitten!

Gertrude cleared her throat once more. "I just want to say: You're welcome."

Aunt Desdemona gasped. Uncle Ansel scoffed. The Lavinias clutched their bichons close to their chests. Grantie Lettuce flared her nostrils.

"What did you say, child?"

"I said, um," Gertrude continued, "you're welcome. 'Cause from when we actually saved you from the worm. You're welcome."

The family had never seen Gertrude act in such a way, i.e., with strength and purpose. They made all sorts of noises: Pshaw! Phooey! AS IF. Only Lavinia-Steve refused to scoff, instead nodding to the Porches with gratitude.

Gertrude nodded back as the Parquettes continued their scornful noises: Tssk. Hahaha! Ugh! Blech.

But underneath all these sounds, there was another sound, a softer sound, the sound of Eugenia and Dee-Dee patting their big sister on the back.

The Porches were riding in a car on their way to the Antiquarium Dock, where a boat would take them to Boston, where a bigger boat would take them to New York, where an even bigger boat would take them to London, where a smaller boat would take them to town in coastal France, where they would board a train in non-coastal Germany, where they would take a car around the rim of a frozen lake to the top of a mountain in Austria, where they would rot in a boarding school until they turned sixteen.

Uncle Ansel drove them in his gleaming red car. He had never had a conversation with the Porches before, but he chose this moment, when they were clutching their suitcases and silently crying, to tell them all about the wonderful world of cuff links.

"You know, a cuff link is like a diamond necklace—but for the sleeve. There are different kinds, of course, and they all say something different. The fixed back says, 'I have an important job!' while the chain style says, 'I come from money and don't need a job!' And of course, each plays differently in the context of the pocket square—"

He stopped at a stoplight and pulled out his map.

"Oh, toad, I missed the darn turn for the toad-darn dock! Toad it!" He threw the map into the passenger seat.

Gertrude glanced sideways at her sisters. It seemed they were all thinking the same mischievous thing. "Um, I think I know where it is," she said. "You actually have to go back around and up Croissant Boulevard, by the cemetery."

It would be wrong to leave forever without at least saying goodbye.

The car sputtered up the hill, past the cemetery. "Well, I don't think this is the way to the dock either!" Ansel fumed.

"We're very close," Gertrude said, and bade him turn left into the cul-de-sac at Mysterium Way.

The street was lined with the same bramble bushes, the same abandoned lots, the same suggestions of what once had been houses, and then, at 231, there was...

NOTHING.

Millicent's house was gone. There was only a hole in the grass where the foundation had been. Had it been burned? Had it been ransacked to the studs by the angry mob? Was Millicent alright? Would they ever see her again? Was she even alive?

The sisters sprang from the car and searched the meadow for some sign, some clue, perhaps one of her famous notes. They scoured the scorched wreckage, finding nothing but ash and bits of broken glass and tattered linen.

"This is no time for lollygagging in random meadows, ladies—the boat is leaving in ten minutes!" Uncle Ansel called.

The Porches looked at one another with trembling chins and moped back to the car.

Uncle Ansel sped away from the former grounds of the short-lived Millicent Quibb School of Etiquette for Young Ladies of Mad Science, while its one-time pupils clung to one another in the back seat, wishing for a different ending.

Three torturous weeks later...

The Versagenschule (School for Failures) was a giant castle of sandstone perched on a snowy white peak in the Austrian Alps, next to a frigid mountain lake.

The Porches arrived at nighttime. The stars shimmered on the surface of the lake, and they could see their breath in the frozen air, even though it was mid-June.

The doors of the castle were flanked by two burning torches and two Doberman pinschers, whose perfectly black fur gleamed blue in the moonlight, and whose lips flared in a smirk on one side, just enough to show the corner of one perfectly sharp Doberman tooth.

The dogs growled at the Porches as they passed through the behemoth wooden doors, which were covered in iron spikes longer than their arms.

Inside the main hall of the cavernous castle, cold fires burned in all the marble fireplaces, fireplaces flanked by—you guessed it—more Doberman pinschers.

They were greeted in the main hall by the headmaster of the Versagenschule, Dr. Klaus Van Hundfreund, which means "dog-friend" in German. He was a tall, sinewy man with white hair to his shoulders, tiny spectacles, and a thin scarf wrapped around his neck.

"We have been expecting you," he said in his heavy German accent, which echoed from the vaulted stone arches overhead. "I am Dr. Hundfreund, but you can just call me Dr. Hundfreund."

The Porches were heavy with the filth of weeks of travel by boat and boat and boat and boat and train and car, but still they trudged dutifully behind Dr. Hundfreund to their new room, which was located at the top of three separate spiral staircases of stone, each one narrower than the last.

The room was a damp stone cell, with only a small round window in the wall and a small round window in the door. The Porches couldn't see but a few feet in front of them, so thick were the clouds of frozen breath puffing from their mouths and noses.

"I will leave you to get settled," he said. "Then in the morning we will begin the delicious process of delving deep into your psyches and finding out why they're wrong, and how to fix them."

He locked the door behind him, leaving the children to shiver in a huddle.

"I guess this is where we live now," said Eugenia.

The sisters all felt like their chests were filled with dead ferns. How could it end like this?

Still, Eugenia reached into her suitcase and pulled out the textbooks Millicent had given them during their training: *Gemistry for Fools*, *Fryzzics Is Fun!*, and *Unnaturalism and You*.

"How did you get those past the dogs?!" Gertrude said, laughing. As they had stepped off the gondola that had carried them across the frozen lake, Dr. Hundfreund had ordered that the sisters' luggage be sniffed by the Dobermans "for weapons, such as books."

"I wrapped them in Taffetteen," Eugenia replied. "No Doberman can sniff through Taffetteen."

The young mad science students happily petted the dusty pages of their textbooks.

They spoke not of the mysteries that lingered in the air: What had become of Millicent Quibb? Why did Millicent choose the three of them for her school? Were all of their mothers really garlic farmers named Pookie? Would they ever get home? What would Majestina DeWeen do next, and who on earth would stop her?

But these were questions for another time. The sisters had only to huddle together through that cold night—to read, to hope.

"We will not rot in this gourdforsaken school," said Eugenia. "When the time is right, we will return to Antiquarium, and we will fight."

"I think I'll shore up Talon Sharktūth's vault so that it can never be opened," said Dee-Dee. "Yeah. I already have an idea about how to do it."

"Good. But for now, we will study," Gertrude said with a lump in her throat, a lump that felt like despair and hope all wrapped up together. "For Millicent."

For Millicent.

Meanwhile, under that same moonlight, on the perimeter of the frozen Austrian lake, a fly sat in wait.

Well, a Fly*cycle*.

Next to the vehicle, a woman in a filthy lab coat and hair like a blooming onion shivered under a pine tree, cursing the cold.

She would have given the crickets in her pocket for a slice of hot pizza, but there were more pressing concerns, namely, rescuing her students from the clutches of the Dobermans.

Her frozen breath swirled and glinted in the moonlight. She puffed three times, sending three rings of breath from her lips, like three smoke signals, one for each of her pupils, who had a lot of work to do.

"Sit tight, my pupeels," she whispered. "Professor Quibb is coming."

THE END

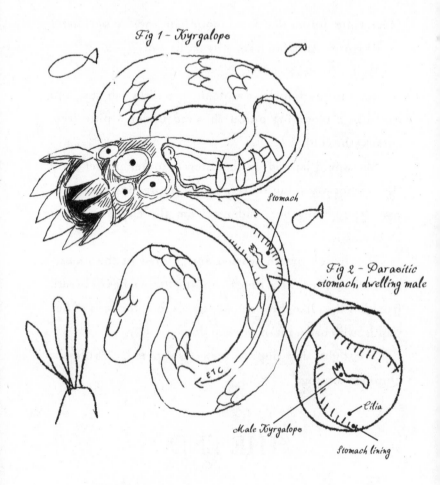

Fig 1 - Kyrgalops

Stomach

Fig 2 - Parasitic
stomach, dwelling male

ETC

Male Kyrgalops

Cilia

Stomach lining

The male of the species lives as a
parasite in the stomach of the female,
never growing larger than a hamster.

EPILOGUE

UNDER THE MOONLIGHT, a worm emerged from the sea: a worm with four crossed eyes, slick red scales, and gnashing mouth parts. The worm slopped forth from the sweet summer waters of Rhodechusetts Bay and wriggled through the sandy dunes. It writhed across grassy lawns, through croquet hoops, over cobblestone sidewalks, and under streetlamps to the darkened fairgrounds, where his wife had writhed and caused a scene one fortnight ago, before being ridden off into the sea. The worm was small, about the size of a hamster, but his mouth could crunch through diamonds. He was tired of living as a parasite in her stomach—he wanted to see the world, to finish what she started! Mr. Kyrgalops, minuscule but mighty, bared his chunky rock-teeth and began gnashing away at the metal door of Talon Sharktūth's vault, bite by tiny bite, slowly and surely. He would be done by morning—and by then it would be too late.

AFTERWORD

CONGRATULATIONS! You've reached the end!
Go get yourself a slice of pizza to celebrate. Of course, you
may have found yourself in a quandary: You wish to know
what happens next. For this, you must somehow find the
second book, which should answer questions such as: Will
the children escape the Austrian prison? What will the KRA
do with Talon Sharktūth's vault now that it's been opened?
Who is the leader of the KRA? Where did I put my pass-
port? Book two will address all these questions, except for
the last! I'll see you there—if you dare!

—G. Edwina Candlestank, Sign Out.

APPENDIX A

THE FIELDS OF MAD SCIENCE

Unnaturalism—the study of unnatural animals
Fryzzics—the building of impossible machines
Gemistry—the study of impossible substances
Whatany—the study of bizarre plants
Chimerology—the behavior of disturbing bats
Viology—the creation of monsters, primarily for
        military use★
Cyanology—the research of poisons★
Animosity—the science of mind control★
Krenetics—the study of reanimation★

★ OUTLAWED.

APPENDIX B

PHYLUM ANNELIDA: THE WONDERFUL WORLD OF WORMS!

There are over 22,000 species of worm in the phylum Annelida! The thing they have in common is that their bodies are organized into segments, which are separated by little membranes called *septa*. They are grouped into different classes: the Polychæta, which are sea worms; the Oligochæta, which are earthworms; and the Hirudinea, which are leeches.

The polychætes live in water and are covered in bristles, like this one, the SANDWORM, which uses its bristles to burrow in wet sand, or this one, the GIANT TUBEWORM, which can survive in deep sea ocean vents on a diet of sulfurous bacteria!

The oligochætes live on land and move segment by segment, like the common EARTHWORM, or the AFRICAN GIANT EARTHWORM, which can grow to be twenty-two feet long!

The Hirudinea live mostly in fresh water, like this one, the MEDIC-INAL LEECH, which has been used by doctors to draw blood for thousands of years—and is still used today! In the 1800s, bloodletting with leeches was so popular that they even had leech FARMS—and there are still leech farms today! Look out, Old McDonald!

Acknowledgments

G. Edwina Candlestank would like to thank:

- The Pizza Association of America, for promoting the interests of pizza, domestically and abroad.

- Mr. Bookman, for being mean to me.

- Pencils, for being pencils.

- Jennifer Turtles.

- My neighbor Sandra, who accidentally smashed my viola and freed me from a life of orchestral misery.

- The Porch Sisters, for giving me permission to pen their tale.

Kate McKinnon would like to thank:

- Erika Turner: Your brilliance and good heart are in every paragraph of this book.

- Alvina Ling, Megan Tingley, Roddyna Saint-Paul, Mishma Nixon, Karina Granda, and Sasha Illingworth, for all their time and support and wisdom.

- Alfredo Cacares, for his exquisite art.

- Jackie Abbott, who was there with the Porches at the beginning.

- Brian Steinberg, without whom I could do nothing.

- Alan Sone, my friend in the world

- My sister, Emily Lynne, the greatest of life's offerings.